P9-CKG-720

EAMON KELLY

IN MY FATHER'S TIME

THE MERCIER PRESS
Dublin & Cork

THE MERCIER PRESS
4 Bridge Street, Cork
25 Lower Abbey Street, Dublin 1

© Eamon Kelly, 1976

ISBN 0 85342 457 8

IN MY FATHER'S TIME was written and devised for the stage by Eamon Kelly. It was first presented at the Peacock Theatre on 23 June 1975, with the author in the part of the Storyteller.

It was directed by Michael Colgan

CONTENTS

To Bat Shea who told me my first story

CHAPTER ONE

BEYOND THE HORIZON

My father never took off his hat except when he was going into bed and into Mass, and my mother said he slept in the two places. At that time every man covered his head. There was respect for the brain then.

As well as covering the head the hat is a handy receptacle. If you are caught short you can give a feed of oats to a horse out of a hat. You can gather apples in the orchard or bring in new laid eggs from the hayshed. In fact, you could nearly put a hen hatching in a hat. . . well, a bantam or a guinea hen.

Headgear gives a man authority. The popes and kings and bishops know this. They always cover their heads when they have something important to say. And where would the storyteller be without his hat when he sits at the fireside to tell a story?

In the long winter nights long ago, the talk'd often turn to some great man who was in the world one time. In our house we'd often talk of Aristotle. Of course the old people had a more homely name for him. They used to call him Harry Stottle. He was a great schoolmaster, and the way he used to teach was walking around the fields so the pupils could be thinning turnips or making hay while they were learning their lessons. In those days great store was

5

set by the pupil's knowing the name and the nature of everything that flew and everything that ran, of everything that grew, and everything that swam. But the old people held that despite all his great knowledge, there were three things Harry Stottle could not understand. And these were, the ebb and flow of the tide, the work of the honey bee, and the fleetness of a woman's mind—exceeds the speed of light!

There were these two Kerrywomen. . . They met on the road one day. One was going to town and the other was coming from town, this now was away back in 1922 when the I.R.Ayes were fighting the I.R.Ah. And all the bridges were blown down. So after a heavy day's rain you'd wet more than your toes fording the river!

The woman going to town, who was on the small side, said to the woman coming from town:

'Were you in town what time is it what price are eggs is the flood high?'

As quick as lightning the woman coming from the town said:

'I was three o'clock one and fourpence up to my arse girl!'

Agus ag trácht dúinn ar uisce, as the man said when he got the half of whiskey at the wake, the Ceannaí Fionn used to sail the watery seas between Iveragh and the continent of Europe long before the Danes discovered Ireland. He used to take over what'd keep you warm on the outside and bring back what'd keep you warm on the inside. He used trade wool for wine. Not a bad swop!

The Ceannaí Fionn's right hand man was Cluasach Ó Fáilbhe, and like Harry Stottle, for they were long headed men, they wondered greatly where the

6

tide went to when it was out and where it came from when it was in. And often on their journeys to and from France and Spain they looked out over the Atlantic Ocean, and they wondered too what was behind that horizon, for at that time no one knew. So they went to find out, but the horizon always remained the same distance in front of 'em. After many months they came back nearly demented from hunger and thirst, although 'tis said all great explorers at that time took enough provisions to last them for seven years going, seven years coming and seven years going astray. They came back and this was the story they told.

'One day they saw a great hole in the middle of the ocean and the sea on all sides pouring down into it.

' "Ah ha," says the Ceannaí Fionn, "we know now! That's where the tide goes to when it is out. But where in the devil does it come from when it's in?" He hadn't the words out of his mouth when an almighty pillar of water shot up out of the hole bringing with it broken ships and every kind, class, form and description of wreckage.

' "That," said the Ceannaí Fionn, "is where the tide comes from when it's in!" A wall of water as high as Mangerton mountain drove the ship westward before it till finally they came to a wall of brass. The sailors hit the wall with their oars and so loud was the report that all the fish stuck their heads up out of the sea. I suppose they thought it was dinner-time!

'They sailed along the wall till they came to a breach high up in it. Now, as sailors are knacky with ropes, they made a rope ladder, threw it up and the Ceannaí Fionn sent up a sailor to see what was at the other side of the horizon. When the sailor got to the top of the wall he gave a great crow of delight and jumped down the other side. Now they had only three sailors on board the ship, so the third fellow got a tight warning, to come back and tell what was at the other side. *Mo léir!* When the third sailor got to the top of the wall he nearly hopped out of his skin with delight and turning his head he said:

' "*Críost go deo!* Did I ever think I'd live to see it!" '

And giving vent to one father and mother of a great yehooo he jumped down the other side.

'Now if the Ceannaí Fionn and Cluasach Ó Fáilbhe were ever again to see Iveragh they knew they'd have to pull down the rope. This they did. And what was behind the wall? Nothing would convince the people who heard the tale but what the sailors saw was women. The Ceannaí Fionn said no. That he had plenty of time to reflect on it and his belief was, that what the sailors saw was the face of God. His belief was that the world was not made all in one slap, all in one week like we were told. Even the eastern half of it would be too big a job for that.

'His belief was, that the brass wall was a sort of hoarding the Almighty put up to keep out the sea while he was finishing the western half of the world! And very likely!

'If they didn't see what was at the other side of the horizon, Cluasach Ó Fáilbhe got a glimpse of another world and this is how it happened. On their way home they were often hungry and they used to throw out the anchor and do a bit of fishing. One day when they went to pull in the anchor they couldn't, so Cluasach Ó Fáilbhe said he'd go down to see what was holding it. He took a deep breath and down with him along the chain to find that the anchor was hooked under the lintel of a door. He went into the house and there inside was, oh! A beautiful young girl.

' "Oh, Cluasach," she said, "I'm watching you every day passing above in the ship. I'm out of my mind in love with you and will you marry me?"

' "All right," said Cluasach, "I will. But I'd like to go home first and talk to my mother."

' "If you go home," she said, "you'll have to give me your solemn promise that you'll come back again, and if you break that promise," she said, "and if you are ever again on the sea, I'll go up and bring you down myself, for I can't live without you!" She had it bad!

'Cluasach gave her his promise and he disentangled the anchor from under the lintel of the door and up the anchor flew bringing him with it. He told the Ceannaí Fionn about the beautiful woman in the house below.

' "Don't mind her," says the Ceannaí Fionn, "You'd get your death from rheumatics living down in that damp old place!"

'He came home and he told his mother, and the mother wouldn't hear of it either. Marrying foreigners! What did he think! She kept him off the sea, from that out—it was no more ships for Cluasach. Time wore on and he couldn't get the image of this beautiful woman out of his mind. One day the men were playing football below in the strand. One awkward fellow kicked the ball into the tide, and Cluasach, forgetting himself, went in after it. And there she was inside the waves waiting. She threw

9

her two hands around him and brought him away
down with her, down under the sea, down to Tír
Fó Thinn. And he never came back, and I suppose
he married her, but he used to send a token. Every
May Eve, for fifty years after, the three burnt
sparks used to come into Trá Fraisc. Didn't he live
a long time down there with her! Marriage never
shortened a man's life if he meets the right woman.'

CHAPTER TWO

GOING TO AMERICA

We lived in an inland parish and the men sitting around my father's fire talking about the Ceannaí Fionn, well, you could count on the fingers of one hand the number of those that ever saw the salt water, except the man going to America. And as the old woman said, 'God help us he saw enough of it!' And I remember a fierce argument cropped up between Batty O'Brien and Coneen Casey, a thin wiry fella, as to how long it was since the first Irishman set foot in America. Weren't they caught short for a topic of conversation!

'Well now,' says O'Brien, a man of large proportions and an historian to boot, 'I can answer that question. The first Irishman to set foot in America was St Brendan the Navigator, for of course 'twas he discovered America. Although he kept his mouth shut about it.'

'How long ago would that be so,' says Casey, 'since St Brendan set foot in America?'

'I can tell you that,' says O'Brien, 'St Brendan was born in Fenit, in Kerry around the year A. D. 500, and he died in Anachuin—I have all this now from the lips of a visiting ecclesiastic—he died in Anachuin about 580. We'll take it now that he did his navigating in his prime, say from 525 to 540.

Add all that up and take it from the year we are living in and it will bring you to within a hen's kick of 1400 years since St Brendan set foot in America.'

'Is that all you know?' says Casey, sort of cool, 'Irish people were going to America before that.'

'Can you prove it?' says O'Brien.

'Faith then, I *can* prove it,' says Casey. 'Otherwise I wouldn't have drawn it down. My own granduncle, Thade Flor was going to America after the famine. In a sailing vessel they were. They were becalmed one evening late, about two hundred miles out from the coast of the Co. Clare. So they threw out the anchor and went to bed for the night—what did they want up for! In the morning there was a stiff breeze blowing. They pulled in the anchor, and do you know what was caught in the hook of it? The wheel of a horse car!'

'And what does that prove?' says O'Brien.

'It proves,' says Casey, 'that Irish people were going to America by road before the flood!'

On the nineteenth day of April
Their gallant ship set sail,
With fifty-five brave Irish lads
True sons of Gráine Mhaoil.
They landed safely in New York
On the nineteenth day of May,
For to meet their friends and relatives
All in the USA.

Their relatives did meet them there
As soon as they did land,
With many a bumper drank their praise
As they clasped hand in hand.
Though some of them had few friends there,

12

Their hearts were light and bold
And by those swaggering Yankees
They could not be controlled!

As six of our brave Irish lads
Were going down Charles Street;
One of these Yankee gentlemen
They happened for to meet.
He brought them to an ale house,
Where he called for drinks galore.
I'm sure such entertainment
They'd never seen before.

The ale it flowed full fast and free
They had a jolly time,
Which was more than they expected
Upon that foreign clime.
But when he thought he had them drunk
The Yankee then did say:
'You are listed in the army now
To fight for America.'

They looked at one another
And then to him made plain:
'It is not for this that we came here
Across the raging main,
But to earn an honest livelihood
As thousands did before,
Who emigrated from their homes
By the dear old Shannon shore.'

Six of these Yankee soldiers
Came dressed without delay.
They said: 'Now lads you must prepare
With us to come away.

This is our esteemed officer
Who listed you complete,
So do not strive for to resist
We can no longer wait.'

The Irish lads hopped to their feet
Which made the Yankees frown;
With every blow that they did strike
They brought a soldier down.
That officer and all his men
They left in crimson gore,
And proved themselves St Patrick's sons
Throughout Columbia's shore.

A Frenchman of great fame had seen
What the soldiers tried to do.
He said: 'I will protect you
From the Yankee criminal crew.
I will take you to Ohio,
Where I have authority,
And keep in employment there
Till you leave this country!'

So now to conclude and finish
Let young and old unite,
And offer up a fervent prayer
Both morning, noon and night
In honour of the Lord above
To help you hold your sway,
And keep you from all danger
When you go to the USA.

And the danger was there. No so much at the
fighting at Bull Run as down the mines in Bute,
Montana. Patey Murrell told me that he heard his

uncle saying that the horses pulling the trolleys down the mines in Bute worked a far shorter day than the men, and the quality of the food they got was better. You see if a horse died of overwork or starvation the Company would have to buy another one, but if a man died there was plenty more waiting outside at the gate. Three times the life of a horse is that of a man, three times the life of a man is that of an eagle, three times the life of an eagle is the life of an oak, three times the life of an oak is the length of time the trace of the ridge and the furrow remains in the ground where land was once cultivated and three times that again'll bring you damn near the end of the world.

But the eagles are gone from Filecannon and gone for a long time now are the men who dug the furrows. I myself saw the tail-end of that great emigration that half emptied the countryside. Often as a small child going to school I called into a neighbour's house to say goodbye to a son or a daughter that was going to America that morning. One kitchen I went into was so dark inside the poor man couldn't shave himself there. There was only a tiny window, if you threw your hat into it, it would be like an eclipse of the sun.

And I have a clear picture in my mind of Pats Pad Duinnín, barefoot in his thick woollen undershirt and long wollen drawers covering him from his Adam's apple down to his ankles—I'd say he got out of that regalia very quick when he hit New York at ninety in the shade. And there he was outside the open door, where he had plenty of light, shaving himself in a looking glass held up by his small brother. So it was:

'Up a bit, up a bit, up a bit. Will you hold it!

15

Down a bit. Where am I now? Tilt it, but don't crookeden it!'

And you know, make it your own case, it was very hard for small Jer D. to judge where his face'd be.

'Hether a bit, over, down! God in heaven I see the clouds but I don't see myself. Up a bit, down a bit. Blast it! Will you hold it straight. I'll look sweet going into the train with a skelp gone outa the jaw!'

He was lathering himself with Ryan's Keltic soap, and after saying goodbye to him I remember wiping the soap off my hand on the backside of my pants as I went down the road to school. I remember too being taken by a neighbour's daughter to a dance—I was only ten at the time!—given in a house in the locality for those going to America. Good fun it was too—the best American wakes they say were in Ireland—and the best Irish wakes in America!

The old people sat around the hearth, drooped and *go brónach*, the red glow of the fire on their faces, their feet keeping time to the music. A set dance was in full swing, the young dancers knocking *fág an bealach* out of the flagged floor. The lamplight throwing their dancing shadows on the whitewashed walls. Down at the butt of the kitchen the musicians were playing. And it was said that these musicians never repeated a tune in the whole run of the night. They had a name for every tune. 'The pigeon on the gate', 'The turkey in the stubbles', 'The cat rambled to the child's saucepan', 'The maid behind the bar', 'Tell her I will'!

If a strange musician didn't know the local names, and the dancers wanted a specific tune, there were rhymes to recall the tune to the fiddler's memory.

16

Like, 'when Hannie got up'!

> Oh when Hannie got up to admire the cups
> She got a stumble and a fall,
> Fell on the chair and broke the ware
> At Thadeneen Andy's ball!

Or another one was:

> Take her away down the quay
> I won't marry her at all today
> She's too tall I'm too small
> I won't marry her at all at all.

In some places those dances were outlawed. They used be raided. In fact a well known Kerry footballer, the first time he saw a flash lamp—carbine they used to have before that, the stink of it!—he told me that he was sitting behind the door on a half sack of bran, a girl on his knee, when the curate flashed a light into his face. And coming at him as it did, all of a sudden out of the dark—especially when he had something else on his mind, he thought it was the end of the world. The effect it had on that man. Put his heart sideways. He never scored after!

All dancing was banned, even in the daylight! Didn't I myself hear Father Walsh saying off the altar:

> I'll put an end to the ball nights. I'll put an end to the porter balls and the Biddy Balls! While there are wheels under my trap I'll go into every corner of the parish. . . I don't care how far in from the public road these. . . balls are held to evade ecclesiastical detection. I'll bring 'em down out of the haysheds! It has come to my ears that young women of marriageable age in

17

this parish have remarked 'How can we get men if we don't go to the balls?' I'll tell 'em how they can get men. I'll tell 'em how! They have only to come round to the sacristy to me any Sunday after Mass and I'll get plenty of men for 'em without any balls. . . a—a bother!

Sentries used have to be posted outside the dance house to raise the alarm when they heard the wheels of Father Walsh's trap—that was before he got the rubber tyres!

One night is gone down in history. Around twelve when the hilarity was at its peak, high jinks in the kitchen and capers in the room, the front door burst open and a sentry rushed in shouting:

'*Tanam an diúcs!* He's down on top of us. He's coming in the *bóthairín!*' Well the back door wasn't wide enough to take the traffic. That for terror! The women's coats and shawls were thrown on the bed below in the room, and in the fuss and fooster to get these, two big women got stuck in the room door. Couldn't go'p or down! Until one clever man put his hand on one of their heads, pushed her down till their girths de-coincided and they were free.

Moll Sweeney was the last one out of the house pulling her shawl around her. Of course when she left the light she was as blind as a bat and who did she run straight into—head on collision—but the parish priest, who was coming in the back way—look at that for strategy to catch 'em all. And Father Walsh to keep himself from falling in the dirty yard, and ruining his new top coat that he had bought that day in Hilliard's Chape Sale, had to put his two hands around Moll to maintain any relationship with the perpendicular. Moll was trying her level best to disentangle herself.

18

'Will you leave go of me! Will you stop I said! Stop I'm telling you. Take your two hands off me whoever you are, and isn't it hard up you are for your hoult and the priest coming in the front door!'

But to come back to the American wake. Between the dances there'd be a song. It would be hard enough to get some of those fellows to sing. One man might be so shy he'd want two or three more standing in front of him, 'Shade me lads!' Or he might run down below the dresser or over to the back door where the coats'd be hanging and before he'd sing he'd draw a coat in front of his face.

> Did ye ever hear tell of Charley the clown?
> He's as useful to Nell as a camel me boys.
> For when she falls drunk he brings her home
>   on his rump
> All the ways from Killarney, boys.

Then by the way that Nell was outside the door he'd mimic Charley talking to her:

'Who is that abroad? Is that you my wife, Nell?
That's me Charley.
And where were you until three o'clock in the morning my wife, Nell?
I was out Charley.
Tis out with boys you've been all night
As I can plainly see,
And if you'll have a son or daughter
They won't belong to me!
So laugh where you are in the corner, boys
For Nellie will shortly barber, boys,
For as sure as you're there she's as mad as a hare,
When she goes and pulls heads with Killaha boys!'

CHAPTER THREE

THE GOBÁN SAOR

As the night wore on there would be many young faces, as the man said, with hunger paling, around the kitchen. That way down in the room refreshments were being served. When it came to my turn to go down, there I saw and heard my first storyteller. A great liar! A stone mason by trade. There he was with his back to the chimney piece shovelling in currant bread and drinking tea out of borrowed delph. When he was finished he blew the crumbs off his moustache, and fixing his eye on a crack over the room door he began:

'A trade,' says he, 'is as good as an estate. A man that knows his trade well can hold his head high in any community, and such a man was the Gobán Saor. He was in the same line of business as myself, he was a stone mason. No word of a lie he had the gift and this is how he got it.

'It so happened one day that the Gobán Saor was out walking when who should he see approaching but an old man with a bag on his back and he bent down to the ground with the weight of it.

'"A very good day to you," says the old man, "are you going far?"

'"To the high field to turn home the cow," says the Gobán, "do you know me?" For the old man

20

was driving the two eyes in through him.

'"I don't," says the old man, "but I knew your father well." With that he left down the bag and sat on top of it.

'"It was ever said," says the old man "that your father would have a son whose name would be the Gobán Saor and this son would build the round towers in Ireland—monuments that would stand the test of time, and the people in future generations would go out of their minds trying to find out why they were built in the first place. One day the Gobán Saor would meet an old man who would be carrying on his back the makings of his famous monuments. Did your father ever tell you that?"

'"He did not," says the Gobán, "for he is dead with long."

'"I think I'll be soon joining him," says the old man, "but I have one job to do before I go. Where would you like to build your first round tower?"

'"I'm going to the high field to turn home the cow," says the Gobán, "so I might as well build it there."

'They went to the high field and the stranger drew a circle with his heel around where the cow was grazing. He opened the bag and they dug out the foundations. Then he gave the Gobán Saor his traps; trowel, hammer, plumb-rule and bob, and he showed him how to place a stone upon a stone. Where to look for the face of the stone and where to look for the bed, where to break the joint, and where to put in thorough bond.

'The wall wasn't long rising, and as the wall rose the ground inside the wall rose with 'em, and they were a good bit up before they thought of the door,

21

and they put in a thin window when they felt like it. When they got thirsty they milked the cow and killed the thirst. The tower tapered in as they went up and when they thought they were high enough the Gobán came out of the top window to put the coping on the tower. By this time the field was black with people all marvelling at the wonder. The Gobán's mother was there and she called out:

'"Who's the young lad on top of the steeple?"'

'"That's your own son," they told her.'

'"Come down!" says she, "And isn't he the limb— and turn home the cow!'

'On hearing his mother the Gobán Saor climbed in the window. The ground inside the tower lowered down with him. When he was passing the door high up in the wall the Gobán jumped, and the cow jumped, and the old man jumped and that was just the jump that killed him and he is buried where he fell, the first man in Ireland with a round tower as his headstone—Daniel O'Connell was the second!

'The Gobán picked up his bag of tricks, and after turning home the cow, his mother washed his shirt and baked a cake, and he went off raising round towers up and down the country. He married, and we are told he had a big family—all daughters, bad news for a tradesman, and an only son. The son, as often happens, turned out to be nowhere as clever as his father, so the Gobán said he'd have to get a clever wife for him and this is how he set about it.

'One day he sent the son out to sell a sheepskin, telling him not to come back without the skin and the price of it—*Craiceann is a luach*. Everyone laughed at the son when he asked for the pelt and the price of it, except one young woman. She

22

sheared the wool of the pelt, weighed it, paid him for the wool and gave him back the pelt and the price of it.

'The Gobán said to the son: "Go now and bring her here to me." The son did and the Gobán put her to another test to make sure. He sent her out with a thirsty old jennet he had, telling her not to let him drink any water unless it was running up hill. She took the jennet to the nearest stream and let him drink his fill. And it ran up hill—up his neck She married the son and was the makings of him!

'When the Gobán Saor had finished the round towers in Ireland, he turned his hand to building palaces, and as every palace he built was always finer than the one before, his fame spread until the King of England sent for him to put up a palace for him, for he wasn't satisfied with the one he had.

'This morning the Gobán Saor and his son set out for England and when they were gone awhile the Gobán Saor said to his son:

'"Shorten the road for me."

And the son couldn't so they turned home. The following morning they set out for England and when they were gone awhile the Gobán Saor said to his son:

'"Shorten the road for me."

The son couldn't so they wheeled around for home a second time. That night the son's wife said to her husband:

'"*I gcúntas Dé a ghrá ghil*, what's bringing ye home every morning. Sure, at this gait of going ye'll never make England."

'"Such a thing," says he, 'every morning when we're gone awhile my father is asking me to shorten the road for him and I can't."

'"Well where were you got," says she, "or what class of a man did I marry! All your father wants is for you to tell him a story and to humour him into it with a skein of a song."

'Oh a fierce capable little woman! *Pé in Éirinn é,* the third morning the Gobán Saor and his son set out for England and when they were gone awhile the Gobán Saor said to his son:

'"Shorten the road for me."

And the son settled into:

> Doh idle dee nah dee am,
> Nah dee idle dee aye dee am,
> Doh idle dee nah dee am,
> Nah dee ah dee aye doh!

And with that they set off in earnest. The son humoured the father into the story of the Gadaidhe Dubh, and they never felt the time going until they landed over in England where the King and Queen were down to the gate to meet 'em.

'"How do I know you're the right man," says the King.

'"Test me," says the Gobán.

So the King pointed out a flat stone up near the top of the old palace, and told the Gobán to cut out a cat with a tail on him on the face of that stone. The Gobán took his magic hammer and aimed it at the stone and up it flew and of its own accord it cut out a handsome cat and it isn't one tail he had but two—the Gobán's trade-mark, a thing that was widely known throughout Europe at the time.

'"Fine out," says the King. "You're elected."

Taking the Gobán to one side and showing him the *cnocán* where he wanted the new palace built.

24

'"And I've the stones drawn and the mortar mixed," says the King.

So the Gobán Saor and his son fell to work and cut the foundations, and it wasn't long at all till the palace was soaring for high, with a hall door fifteen feet off the ground and a ladder going up to it that the King could pull in after him in case of any scrimmage, for there is no knowing how *trí na céile* things were in England at that time.

'Well, when the King saw the way the palace was shaping, he was rubbing his hands with delight, and he was every day saying to the Gobán, was it true that the last palace he built was always finer than anything he ever built before? The Gobán said that was correct.

'"I'm glad to hear it," says the King, "and as sure as you're a foot high the day the palace is finished, there's a surprise in store for you."

'The Gobán was wondering what these words meant and this is how he found out. 'Twas a daughter of Donaleen Dan's that was housekeeping for that King of England at the time his own wife was that way and not able for the work, and every day when the Gobán and his son'd come in to their dinner the two of 'em and Miss Donaleen'd be talking: *Bhí an Ghaeilge go blasta aice siúd, agus is i nGaelige a bheidís ag caint i gcónaí*, and the King of England didn't know no more than a crow what was going on!

'"Bad tidings," says Miss Donaleen this day.

'"That King is stinking with pride, and he's saying now that if the Gobán Saor and his son go off and build another palace for the King of Wales or the King of Belgium, it will be better than his own, and then he won't have the finest palace in the world. So as soon as ever the job is finished he's planning to cut the heads down off the two of ye! That's the surprise you're going to get!" Wasn't it far back the roguery was breaking out in 'em, eroo!

The Gobán slept on this piece of information and in the morning he said to his son:

"'If my plan don't work I can see the two of us pushing *nóiníns* before the hay is tied."

"'*Cuir uait an caint*," says the son. "Here's the King coming."

Along came the King rubbing his hands with delight and he said to the Gobán.

"'Is this now the finest palace in the three Kingdoms."

"'It is," says the Gobán.

"'And tell me," says the King, "is it long until you'll have it finished?"

"'Only to put the coping on the turret," says the Gobán, "but the implement I want for doing that is called the *cor in aghaidh an chaim...*"

"'English that for me," says the King.

"'Tis the twist against crookedness," says the Gobán, "but bad manners to it for a story, didn't I forget it at home in Ireland after me, so I'll hare back for it and bring my son to shorten the road for me."

"'You'll do no such thing," says the King, "you'll stand your ground and I'll send my own son for it." Well, that was that for as we all know there's no profit in going arguing with a King.

'Now at home in Ireland the Gobán's son's wife, that fierce capable little woman, was baking a cake this day when who walked in the door to her but the King of England's son.

"'Such a thing," says he, "I'm from over."

26

'"Is that so," says she. "Is it long from the palace?"

'"'Tis nearly ready now," he said, "only to put the coping on the turret, but they forgot the implement for doing that, 'tis called 'the twist against crookedness'."

'She tumbled to that:

'"You'll find it there in the bottom of the bin." she said, "and if you're not too high and mighty in yourself you can stand up on the chair and stoop down for it."

And if he did, she kicked the chair from under him, knocked him into the bin, banged down the cover and locked it.

'"Ah-ha-dee," says she. "You'll remain a captive in there until my husband and my husband's father'll come home to me, so write out a note to that effect and hand it through the mouse hole!"

He did, and she gave the note to Gobán's pet pigeon, and he knew where to go with it—why wouldn't he! And the plan worked and she hadn't long to wait and she knew who was to her coming up the *bóthairín* when she heard:

> Doh iddle dee nah dee am.
> Nah dee iddle dee aye dee am,
> Doh iddle dee nah dee am
> Nah dee ah dee aye do.'

That stone mason had never been a mile from a spring well, but to hear him talking you'd swear he's been to the moon and back. Going away was the topic on the tip of everyone's tongue that night and the storyteller liked it to be known that he was away himself. This is how he acquainted us of it.

'In my father's time things were slack at the

27

stone masoning and my mother said to me: "Isn't it a fright," says she, "to see a big fosthook like you going around with one hand as long as the next, and why don't you go away and join the DMP's for yourself!"

'They were the old Dublin police, a fine body of men. So I took her at her word and hit for Dublin and the depot, and joined up, and after a *tamall* of hard careering around the barrack square, a solid gounding in acts of parliament and all that I was put into a new uniform and let loose in the city of Dublin!

'My first assignment was public house duty in Parnell Square—kind of a swanky place. I tell you I wasn't long there when I instilled a bit of law and order in them lads with regard to late closing and that. Things rested so. I was this night going along. . . it would be well after half eleven I'd say. When I saw a light coming through the hole in a shutter of a certain establishment. I went up and put my eye to the hole and what was it, you devil, but a line of lads up to the counter with loaded pints! I banged on the knocker and the publican came out. "What's this?" says I, "what class of carry on is this?"

'"Oh Ned," says he, "sure you won't be hard on me."

'"Ned!" says I, "what Ned! I don't know you my dear man, or the sky over you!"

'"I'm a cousin of your own twice removed, I'm a boy of the Connor's from the cove of Sneem!"

'"Jer Dan's son," says I.

'"The very man," says he.

'"Well now," says I, "you could have knocked the cover off my pipe, I never knew you were in Dublin or in the public house trade."

28

"'Oh I am," says he, "come on away in till we try and soften things out."

'Well, seeing that he was a connection and all to that I went in with him, but I must say this much for him. He was not a grasping fellow. I was no sooner in than he cleared the premises, sat me down and landed me out a healthy *taoscán* from the top bottle in the house and told me I'd be welcome at any time which I was!

'I was this night above inside in the cousins with my shoes off toasting my toes to the fire—a smart *smathán* of punch in front of me—we were tracing relative-ships. When around half past twelve the thought was foreshadowed to me that the D. I. might be around on a round of inspection do you see. I stuck the legs into the shoes, mooched out to the front door and there he was coming up along, so I pulled the door after me and 'pretined' to be standing in from the rain. Up he came.

"'Night Ned," says he.

"'Night Officer," says I.

"'Be telling," says he.

"'Nothing to tell," says I, "the publicans in this quarter are living up to the letter of the law."

"'Good," says he, "I'm hearing great accounts about you. Come on and we'll bowl down along."

"'Right," says I, and made a move to go, but couldn't stir a leg. What was it but when I pulled the door behind me the tail of my coat got caught in it, and there I was stuck like a spider to the wall. Wasn't that a nice pucker to be in! If it was raining soup it is a fork I'd have!

"'Have you ere a match?" says I sparring for wind.

'Decent enough he handed me a box of 'em. I

began cutting a bit of tobacco to put in the pipe. All the time racking my brains for a way out of the pucker. With that there was an almighty crack of thunder that nearly rent the heavens.

'"It'll make a dirty night," says I, "and your best plan now'd be to run along home to the little woman for she'll be frightened."

'And they do—about the only thing they're frightened of! That put the skids under him and off he went. Up here you want it, down below for dancing! When he was gone I bent down to try to disentangle myself out of the door when I heard a voice behind me.

'"You didn't give me back my matches." says he. Oh a mean man that same D.I. I was back stone masoning the following week!'

CHAPTER FOUR

GOING TO THE TRAIN

The young people going away to America they'd contribute too to the general hilarity and I remember that night Mick the fiddler told the story about his father and the three travelling tailors.

At that time poor people could only afford meat once a week. And before that again there was a time in the history of Sliabh Luachra when people could only have meat three times a year, at Christmas, Easter and Shrove Tuesday night.

One Sunday, Mick, the fiddler's father, was sitting by the hearth. The spuds were done and steaming over the fire, and at the side of the fire, nesting in the *griosach*, was a small pot, the skillet. In the skillet was a piece of imported bacon called American long bottom bubbling away surrounded by some beautiful white cabbage. For a whole week the poor man had been looking forward to this hour. And you wouldn't blame him if his teeth were swimming in his mouth with mind for it. His wife Mary was laying the table when the front door opened and in walked three travelling tailors, ravenous.

D'réir an seana chultúr, 'twas share and share alike, already Mary was putting out three plates so that the man had to think quick. Mick the fiddler himself was only a small child of about a year and a half running around the floor in petticoats. They wouldn't put any trousers on a little boy at that time until he was five—people were more practical. The father picked him up and began dangling him that way.

'He didn't dance and dance, he didn't dance all day, he didn't. . .' When the tailors weren't looking he whipped a big spud out of the pot and then attracting the tailors' attention he let the spud fall from under the child's clothing into the cabbage and bacon!

You'd travel from here down to see the look on the tailors' faces.

'I'm afraid,' says he letting down the child. . . 'I'm afraid it'll be spuds and salt all round. . . Of course Mary and myself could eat the bacon. After all the child is our own!'

It was common at the time to give those going away a little present. Maybe a crown piece or a half sovereign, happy indeed'd be the one that'd get a golden guinea. As well as that the girls might get wearables. A pair of gloves or the like, and it was usual to give the men a silk handkerchief. You'd see 'em sqeezing it and on opening their hand if it bounced up it was pure silk. Of they'd throw it at the wall and if it clung to the mortar it was the genuine article. And you'd see those handkerchiefs the following morning waving from the train as it went out of sight under the Countess' bridge.

In the morning the horses'd be tackled, and any-one who could afford it'd go to the station. A long line of cars like a wedding drag. How is this the Limerick man remembered it?

The terminus was crowded with folks
   from Everywhere,
They were there from Castleconnell
   and from the Co. Clare,
There were girls there from Limerick
   from Croom and sweet Moroo,
And they all seemed very lonesome
   as they bid their friends adieu.

Lonesome was no name for it. Often I was there
as a child. At that time it would take the young man
going to America eight to ten days to get there in
rickety old ships—you could feel the motion of the
waves under your feet. And then when he landed
over in New York he'd have to work very hard to
put the passage money together to bring out his
brother. That's how 'twas done. John brought out
Tim and Tim brought out Mary. Maybe then he'd
get married and have responsibilities, so when again
would that young man standing there. . . when
again would he come back over the great hump of
the ocean—if ever.

He'd be surrounded on the platform by his
friends, and when the time came for him to board
the train he'd start saying goodbye to those on the
outside of the circle, to his far out relations and
neighbours, plenty of gab for everyone, but as he
came in in the circle, to his cousins, to his aunts
and his uncles, the wit and the words would be
deserting him. Then he'd come to his own family,
and in only what was a whispering of names, he'd
say goodbye to his brothers and sisters. Then he'd
say goodbye to his father, and last of all to his
mother. She'd throw her two arms around him, a
thing she hadn't done since he was a small child
going to school, and she'd give vent to a cry, and

33

this cry would be taken up by all the women along the platform. Oh, it was a terrifying thing for a small child like me to hear. It used even have an effect on older people. Nora Kissane told me she saw a man running down the platform after the train so demented he was beckoning his fist at the engine and shouting:

'May bad luck to you out ole smokey hole taking away my fine daughter from me!'

And there was a widow that worked her fingers to the bone to get the passage money together to send her son to America. A rowdy she wasn't going to be sorry after. A useless yoke, nothing for him but his belly full of whiskey and porter when he could get it, singing in the streets until all hours of the morning. A blackguard that put many a white rib of hair on his mother's head—took three young girls off their road. The devil soften 'em. They were worse to let him.

The woman was not going to go to the station at all to see him off, but when she saw how lonely the parents were parting with their children she thought, 'they'll think me very hard hearted now if I don't show come concern.' And of course when her heart wasn't in it she overdid it. She went over to the window of the train he was standing inside in the carriage, and throwing her hands to heaven she said:

'Oh John, John, John, don't go from your mother! Don't go away, John. Oh you sweet, utter, divine and lovely little God sitting above on the golden cloud why don't you dry up the Atlantic ocean so the ship couldn't sail and take my fine son away from me. John, John, don't go from your mother, John!'

He opened the door and walked out saying:

34

'I won't go at all Mother!' He went down the town and into the first public house and drank his passage! You heard the singing in the street that night! —

You brave Irish people where ere you may be,
Pay attention a moment and listen to me!
Your sons and fair daughters are now going away,
Emigrating in thousands to Amerikay!

Their friends they assemble, their neighbours also,
Their cases are packed all ready to go,
The tears from their eyes are falling like rain
As the horses are starting to go away to the train.

When they go in the carriage you can hear the
    last cry,
There are handkerchiefs waving bidding goodbye,
The wild grief of their parents no words can
    portray
And they cling to their dear ones as the train
    pulls away.

Choo chit choo chow, choo chit choo chow.
Good b. b. b. bye!
Choo chit choo chow, choo chit choo chow.
Good bye Ireland. I'm going to Cork!

CHAPTER FIVE

PEGG THE DAMSEL

Choo chit, choo chow, choo chit, choo chow, choo chit, choo chow. Choo, choo, ch... ch... ch. . . ow! Ch... ch... sssssh! Cork! Glanmire Station. Cork!

Whatever part of Ireland you left that time going to America you have to pass through Cork and then down to Queenstown.

Over here for the boat train. Over here all those for Queenstown. All aboard the boat train! Mind your coat in the door there! All aboard! Choo chit, choo chow. Choo chit, choo chow.

They travelled on for fifteen miles
By the banks of the River Lee.
Spike Island soon came into view,
And the convicts they did see.
They all put up in Mackey's Hotel,
Nine dozen of them or more,
And they sang and danced the whole night long
As they did the night before!

Sweet Kingwilliamstown

My bonny barque bounds light and free
Across the raging foam,
Which bears me far from Innisfail

To seek a foreign shore.
A lonely exile driven neath
Misfortune's coldest frown,
From my loved home and cherished friends
In sweet Kingwilliamstown.

Shall I no more gaze on that shore,
Or climb the mountains high;
Or stray along Blackwater's banks,
I strayed when but a child,
Or watch the sun o'er Knocknabower
Light up the heather brown,
Before he cast his farewell beams
On sweet Kingwilliamstown.

In the morning they'd go out in the tender, out
the harbour to where the ship was waiting. They'd
go on board and sail away, and the last thing they'd
see—often I heard those who came back remark on
it—the last sight of home was the Skelligs Rock,
the half circle of foam at the base of Sceilig Mhichíl.

As here I stand upon the deck
And watch the fading shore,
Fond thoughts arise within my mind
Of friends I'll see no more;
Of moonlit streams and sunny hours
While fast the tears roll down,
Oh God be with you Innisfail
And sweet Kingwilliamstown.

Now that they were gone the people at home sat
back. . . and waited for the money! The first Christmas cards we, as children saw, came from New
York. They had lovely drawings of St Joseph and
the Holy Family, but lovely and all as those drawings were they couldn't hold the candle to the

picture of George Washington—and if George Washington or General Grant weren't inside the crib with the Holy Family there wouldn't be much welcome for the Christmas Card. Indeed I heard of one man who used cut open the letter, shake it, and if a few dollars didn't fall out he wouldn't bother reading it! What bank would change a Christmas card!

But to be fair the money nearly always came to the mother. It was the indoor and outdoor relief—the dole, grant and subsidy of the time. She would put it to good use. It would go to buy the few luxuries they'd otherwise have to do without at Christmas. It would go to improve the house, to put extra stock on the farm, to educate a child—where did the Civil Service come from! And as people got old the money'd go to take out the appendix or to put in false teeth!

Anyone that ever went the road to Killarney couldn't miss Pegg the Damsel's slate house. 'Twas at the other side of the level-crossing, and you couldn't miss that either, for any time I ever went that way one gate was open and the other gate was closed—they were always half expecting a train!

Pegg's house was done up to the veins of nicety—dormer windows out on the roof, variegated ridge-tiles, walls pebble dashed—what you could see of 'em—for they were nearly covered with ivy. In the front garden she had ridges of flowers, surrounded by a hedge, beautifully clipped, you may say the barber couldn't do it nicer, and one knob of the hedge left rise up, and trained to give the effect of a woman sitting down playing a concertina—Pegg herself, of course, for she was a dinger on the box! I tell you if you heard her playing the Verse of

38

Vienna, you'd never again want to turn on the wireless. How is this she had it!

Father Walsh's, Father Walsh's,
    Father Walsh's top coat,
For he wore it and he tore it
    and he spoiled his top coat.
Diddle dee ing dee die doe,
    Diddle dee ing dee die dee,
Diddle dee ing dee die dee,
    Diddle dee ing dee die doe.

She was brilliant! Of all the posies in Pegg's garden the roses took pride of place. She had 'em there of every hue—June roses, tea roses, ramblers and climbers. Now, at the back of Pegg's house there was a farmer living called Ryan, and he had a goat running with the cows. And a very destructive animal he was too. He came the way and he knocked into the garden and he sampled the roses, and he liked 'em, and he made short work of 'em!

Pegg complained the goat to Ryan. 'And what do you want him for?' says she, 'with ten cows, sure 'tisn't short of milk you are!'

'Ah, 'tisn't that at all,' says Ryan, 'goats are said to be lucky, and another thing they'll ate the injurious herb and the cows'll go their full time—if ye folly me? You needn't be in Macra na Feirme to know that!'

'You'll be doing full time,' says Pegg, 'if that goat don't conduct himself, for I'll have you up before the man in the white wig.'

'Play tough, now,' says Ryan, a man afraid of his life of litigation for it can lighten the pocket. 'I've a donkey chain there and I'll shorten it down to make a fetters for the goat.'

Which he did! But when the goat got the timing of the chain, like the two lads in the three-legged race, he was able to move as quick with it as without it.

Now, that was the same year Pegg married the returned Yank. . . or was it? 'Tis so long 'go now... everything is gone away back in my poll. 'Twas! A man that went in a fright for fancy shirts—and they do. One day is all he'd keep the shirt on him. Look at that for a caper! The poor woman kept going washing!

This morning she rinsed out his red shirt and put it outside on the hedge to dry. That was all right, no fault until the goat bowled the way, and handicapped and all as he was, he broke into the garden— attracted by the colour, I suppose! And Pegg the Damsel opened the front door just in time to see the white button of the left cuff disappearing down the goat's throttle.

There was no good in calling the Yank, he was in blanket street waiting for the shirt to dry! All night work he had in New York and he used to sleep during the day, but as he had no night work here he used to sleep day and night!

She chased the goat with the broom and he made off up the railway from her. He ran down the slope and when he was crossing over the tracks, well, 'twouldn't happen again during the reign of cats, didn't one link of the chain go down over the square headed bolt that's pinning the rail chair to the sleeper. He was held there a prisoner, he couldn't lead or drive, and what was more he heard the train whistling—'twas coming now. Wasn't that a nice pucker for a goat to be in, and if I was there and if ye were there, we'd lose our heads, but the goat didn't. What did he do? He coughed up the red shirt and flagged down the train!

CHAPTER SIX

SHROVETIME

Pegg's Yank, the man in the red shirt, came home on a trip and made a match with Pegg. Pegg was a monitor—well a junior assistant mistress, so he had jam and jam up on it!

A lot of young people going away at that time looked upon America as a place or state of punishment where some people suffered for a time before they came home and bought a pub, or a farm or married into land or business. . . like Pegg's Yank. A fair amount succeeded. If you walked around the country forty years ago every second house you'd go into either the man, or his wife, had been to America.

Many is the young woman came back—well she wouldn't be young then after ten years in New York, but young enough!—and married a farmer, bringing with her a fortune of three or four hundred dollars. Then, if the farmer had an idle sister—and by idle there I don't mean out of work! —the fortune was for her. Then she could marry another farmer, or the man of her fancy, that's how the system worked, and that fortune might take another idle sister out of that house and so on! So that the same three hundred dollars earned hard running up and down the steps of high stoop houses

in New York City could be the means of getting anything up to a dozen women under the blankets here
in Ireland! And all pure legal!

There was no knowing the amount of people
that'd get married at that time between Chalk Sunday and Shrove Tuesday. But quare times as the
cat said when the clock fell on him, no one at all'd
get married during Lent, or the rest of the year. So,
if you weren't married during Shrove Tuesday night
you could throw your hat at it. You'd have to
wait another twelve months, unless you went out
to Skelligs where the monks kept old time. Indeed
a broadsheet used to come out called the Skelligs
List—it used be shoved under the doors Ash Wednesday morning. Oh, a scurrilous document in
verse lampooning all those bachelors who should
have, but didn't get married during Shrovetime.

> There's Mary the Bridge
> And Johnny her boy friend,
> They are walking out now
> For twenty one springs!
> There's no ditch nor no dyke
> That they haven't rolled in—
> She must know by now
> The nature of things!
>
> 'Oh Johnny,' says she,
> 'Do you think we should marry
> And put an end for all time
> To this fooster and fuss?'
> 'Ah Mary,' says he,
> 'You must be near doting.
> *Who* do you think
> Would marry either of us!'

Who indeed! But the matchmaker was there to
put the skids under 'em. That's one thing we had in

43

common with royality, matchmaking—of course
the dowries weren't as big!

Why then there was a match made for myself
one time, and it is so long ago now that I won't be
hurting anyone's feelings by telling ye the comical
way things turned out.

At that time anyone that had the notion of
giving the place to his heir, be it son or daughter,
would make that fact known down at the chapel
gate and elsewhere coming up to Shrove. And Sylvie
na Scolb was among those that gave vent to such a
rumour in the year I'm alluding to. Sylvie's way of
living was small, grass of a couple of cows, but as
he was a thatcher he wasn't depending on it.

An only daughter is all he had for the place, and
clever enough, faith, he was all out to get a tradesman for a *cliamhain isteach*, so he ran an account
to our house, and the old people here at the time
said nothing could be lost by entering into nego-
tiations. Word was sent back that we'd meet the
other party in Coiner's snug the coming Saturday.

Come Saturday, and it was my first glimpse of
Sylvie. Oh, a cross little wasp of a fellow! Is it any
man that shot his own father-in-law in the leg the
time of the moonlighting! But a great warrant to
drink you may say! For when my father put the
pint in front of him, with the first slug he drove it
below the tops of the church windows, wiped the
froth off his moustache and said: 'Now then!' So
we got down to business. 'No man,' says Sylvie,
"'ll darken my door down of seventy pounds! And
there'll be no twenty pounds down and the rest at
the first christening! A lump sum or nothing.'

'*Cúis gháire chughainn*,' says my father, 'tisn't a
demesne you have—rushes and fellistrums, aren't

44

you getting a man with a trade?'

'And he's getting a good girl!' says Sylvie.

'We didn't see her yet,' says my father. 'Take fifty.'

'I said seventy.'

'Take sixty.'

'Look,' says Sylvie, 'put another five on top of it, and don't anyone hear us haggling here like Sheridans!'

'Twas done and my father called for another round. Sylvie must have got into the wrong trousers coming out in the morning, for he never ventured near the pocket at all. And isn't it the likes of him that'd get on!

'Well,' says Sylvie, viewing me for the first time, 'What night are you coming over to see Béib, Ned?'

'Whatever night ye are eating the gander,' says I.

'Aiting the Gander' was a very enjoyable pre-nuptial function that went on to give the parties a chance of getting acquainted.

'The Gander', says Sylvie, 'will be Thursday, so let ye come early and walk the land.'

We all sailed over Thursday, walked the land, inspected the stock, 'twas aisy count 'em, three cows and a jennet! Counted the cow tyings in the stall—extra cow tyings'd be put in during the making of a match. They'd be taken out and more with 'em when the old age pension officer'd come!

Then we went in to see Béib. Well, as nice a girl as you could wish to see, but very shy and distant in herself. She hadn't a word for the priest only 'Yes' and 'No', and inclined to call me 'Sir'!

We all sat in to roast goose and there was dancing after, and when Béib and myself took the floor what did the fiddler strike up, out of pure devilment, but the Mason's Apron. We had the sport of Cork and Béib said she thought she liked me, and I couldn't say anything with the crowd around.

We were in town again the coming Saturday doing the bindings—the marriage agreement. All the signing! You'd think it was the Treaty of Versigh! The double deed came in at the time, and the two of our names were put in the land. The sixty-five pounds was paid down—to the Attorney for the time being in case of any crux. A proviso was put in for fear Sylvie and the missus'd take to the room. The usual proviso was that the old couple'd get their full needs of combustibles—milk, turf, butter and eggs, a seat in the car to Sunday Mass, or any other big excursion like going to town to turn the bit of money. And the wedding was to be the coming Tuesday—Shrove Tuesday.

I went to bed early Monday night in the room below the kitchen. Our house was all on the ground in a hollow and it was just as well for the wind was rising, and it was cold enough to snow— and as the man said, it looked as if it might be a white wedding!

I found the night awful long! The cock crew and it never dawned. The old people got up and made tae. They thought the night awful long. I got up. We all went to bed again. Well, between the ups and the downs I woke up in the latter end—I think 'twas the cock woke me—to see a chink of light coming in at the top of the room window. I jumbed out, ran down and opened the door. What was it, you diggle, but a wall of snow up to the eaves of the house! The clock was stopped... I didn't know where I was. I dolled up in a jiffy and tunnelled my way out through the snow and made every near-way for the chapel. There was no one there, but knowing women I made allowances. I waited on.

'You're getting very devout!' says the parish clerk coming up behind me. 'Where were you yesterday?'

'Getting ready for today,' says I.

'That you mightn't sin,' says he. 'Isn't *today* Ash Wednesday. Don't you see the women coming in for the ashes!'

That explained it! I knew there was something unnatural in having to get up five times the one night—for a man of my age! I was in bed since Monday. But when I explained the thing to the injured party that I was snowed under for two nights and a day. . . they wouldn't hear of it.

'Clear,' says Sylvie, 'or I'll make a strainer of you with the double barrel.'

And of course Béib wouldn't look at the same side of the road at me from that out. I was free and she was idle for another year! But it didn't set me back much, for before Lent was out I went building gate piers to a place called The Lots, where I met the little woman that's with me since. If Béib was nice Juil took the cake, and I married her for love and in that way started the fashion in this locality.

But there were plenty of love matches that time too and plenty of love-making. How you'd know that is by the bluebells in the wood and the long grass on the slopes of the railway. They used to come in for a bit of flattening! That was all right in the summer of course, but coming home from a ball night in the middle of winter, you might be conveying home a little pusher and she might say to you, 'I know what you mean but the grass is wet.' Well, there was nothing for it then only to go up on a hayshed. And if you were a clever young lad you'd pick a hayshed where the dog knew you, otherwise the farmer'd be out and leave the print of the four prongs of the dung fork in your back-side—that'd bring down your temperature! He wasn't worried about the damage you'd do to the ten commandments, but that you might set fire to his hay.

You'd never think it now, but I spent a few nights in a hayshed myself. The first time I was only fifteen, fair play to me! There was a friend of mine, much older than me conveying this pusher home from a ball night—four o'clock in the morning. She had a sister coming in the way like, so I was only giving him a helping hand. The sister was as young as myself, a pure greenhorn—after a bout of tickling we fell asleep!

But it was always said those made matches worked well. Although I did hear a travelling man say. . . There used to be a bed for the poor in nearly every house that time—*leabaidh na mbocht*—if it wasn't there the man of the house would go out in the haggard and bring in a number of sheaves of oats and spread 'em on the floor. . . two for a pillow. Then there was an old linen sheet, kept for the purpose, to cover the straw. At bedtime the traveller would lie on that, his marshal cloak around him like Sir John Moore, but unlike Sir John Moore he'd be up with the crack of dawn in the morning and he'd have all the straw out in the yard and the floor swept.

These men were always welcome for they were great carriers of news and gossip, and I heard one of them say that he knew for a positive fact that the morning of a wedding a different woman was substituted at the altar steps. I never heard it myself and I remember drawing it down to Master Buckley.

'It never happened,' says he, 'only more of this bla'guarding put out to ruin our reputation!'

I don't know. The travelling man told us of another case which he saw with his own two eyes. And by the same token it was a man home from Springfield Mass. that married into this place where there was an only daughter—oh very well to do. All saddle horses that were in the wedding drag. There was a race back to the house every man with his woman up behind him—riding *cúlóg*. Very romantic, he said, but awful dangerous over stoney ground. Some of them were thrown off, but I suppose that was part of the fun. He was at the wedding that night. We asked him was he invited. No, he said, he strawed. And that's a thing used to take place, if you weren't invited to a wedding, you could see the inside of the house for a while by strawing it. The straw was a disguise, and this was how it was done. You'd make a straw rope, a *súgán, a méaróg*, it was made with the finger. A stretch of the hands would be long enough. Two fellows'd hold that. Then you'd get clean scotched straw, eight or ten laces at a time, attach it to the rope falling to the ground all along until you had a fine curtain of straw. You tied that around your middle and it covered you all the way to the floor.

Then you made a second *méaróg*. You took the laces of straw as before, and there was a very clever knot for fixing the laces to the rope. The way it was done the second knot kept the first one in position and so on. When the curtain of straw was ready you lifted it up tied it on like a cape and it covered you from the shoulders down as far as it would go. Now, you made a third straw rope, it was a three piece suit, fixed the straw along it, and when it was complete you brought the rope around, put a knot on it leaving a circle just big enough to go down over your head. Then bringing all the straw in to a point you made a tall cone-shaped hat. When you tied the straw six or eight inches down from the top the hat looked like a small stook of oats, or maybe more like an indian's wigwam, only they'd be the *suarachy* indians that'd go into it! Then you'd lift it up, let it fall down over your head and you were completely covered in straw, except, as the man said, you could see out but you couldn't be seen in.

There was a damn nice cuck on top of the hat, and the captain of the straw-boys would part that in two places making three cucks on top of his hat. This was so it would be easy to pick him out in the crowded wedding house. He gave the orders. He had his men numbered, there might be ten of 'em in a batch, because if he called out their names in the house they'd be known. You'd have to be very wary inside there and keep an eye on your comrade in front and hope the fellow behind kept an eye on you. The danger was that some blackguard with the signs of drink on him might redden a splinter in the fire and set fire to the straw!

After the batch of strawboys were admitted to the wedding house the captain, altering his voice, would wish the newly married couple joy. He and his men'd be given a drink, and in return they'd dance a set. This payment they gave with a heart and a half. Idle women'd be mad to go out dancing

50

with the strawboys. The great fun for them'd be trying to find out who the men were, poking their fingers through the straw masks to see who was behind them. When the music was in full swing there was nothing as lovely as all that whirling straw under the light of the lamp.

In the old days of the mud floor the door'd be taken off the *bacáns* and two strawboys'd dance the challenge hornpipe on top of it. That was before the oil lamp, and to brighten things up the other strawboys would redden bog dale splinters in the fire and ring the dancers with a blaze of light. As well as dancing a man whose number was called out by the captain might give a bit of a dust-up on the box, or play the flute. The travelling man said when his number was called he told the story of Bláthnaid the daughter of the King of the Isle of Man. The story was so well received, and he was a dinger to tell one, that the bridegroom asked the storyteller to remain on for the rest of the night as his special guest. This he did, and when his comrades went out he took off his straw suit and, as he said himself, sat with the select.

It was a great wedding. The man home from Springfield Mass. spared no expense in food or drink. At that time it was a great boast to have it to say 'we danced till daylight' and weddings'd last the night and maybe into the following day. Now, it was only natural to expect that the newly married couple might like to be alone for a while. What they used to do in some places was to go down in the room and put the press to the door, or run upstairs.

Upstairs they went in this place for it was a slate house. They'd be gone for a while, but the hilarity'd be kept up, no notice taken. People had enough upbringing at the time not to remark on what was natural. About an hour after the man from Springfield Mass. walked down the stairs, his face as white as chalk, a wild *sceón* in his eyes and he cursing under his breath the day he ever put foot inside the door. He walked out, his brother had to go up and get his clothes, for it seems the one he married was not a proper woman!

God bless the mark! 'What would you do if the kettle boiled over? What would you do but to fill it again. What would you do if you married a soldier? What would you do but to marry again.' But that man never married again, and people in authority who couldn't be without knowing, never lifted as much as a little finger to dissolve that unnatural union. And the money he brought into that house as *cliamháin isteach* was never paid back to him, and his people and her people used to belt each other black and blue over it every fair day. The old people always said that God could knock you sideways for laughing at a man in misfortune, but we couldn't help smiling in our minds for we knew that the man from Springfield Mass. would never have found himself in that pucker if he gave a few nights up on a hayshed with her!

CHAPTER SEVEN

BLÁTHNAID
THE DAUGHTER OF
THE KING OF THE ISLE OF MAN

When Bláthnaid's father, the King of the Isle of Man, found out who his daughter was going with he locked her up in the top room and hunted Cú Chulainn off the island.

Cú Chulainn came home and told his uncle Concubhair Mac Neasa the way he was insulted. And Concubhair, being King of the north at the time, rising up, he said:

'Call out the Army and we'll go over and soften the wool in that lad!'

That night under cover of darkness Cú Chulainn and his men set sail for the Isle of Man but when they landed over there, there was a huge wheel of flame circling the King's fortress and they couldn't go near it.

Now, who should be passing at the time but Cú Rí Mac Dáire, the King of Kerry—an almighty big man, as big as any five facing in Rathmore Mass. There he was in disguise whatever he was up to in the Isle of Man. When Cú Rí saw the pucker the northmen were in, he ran over and met the wheel of flame with one flying kick and sent it soaring up into the stars and I make out it is up there all the time wheeling around. Russians *mar eadh!*

Now that the road was clear Cú Chulainn's men charged into the fort killing all round 'em. They broke down the door of Bláthnaid's room and set her free. Then they went off looting through the palace and there was no end to the riches they found gold and jewels, and they brought it all to one place and made a big heap of it in the middle of the floor. And the soldiers were going over and picking up a jewel, polishing it on their sleeve and hooking it on their belts, when Cú Chulainn said, 'Where are ye're manners, or who did the greatest *gaisge* here tonight?' And they said that big man there in disguise that kicked the wheel of flame up into the stars. 'Right!' says Cú Chulainn, 'then it is only fair that he should get the finest jewel; stand back and let him have his pick!' Cú Rí Mac Dáire, the King of Kerry, walked over to where Bláthnaid was standing, picked her up and walked out the door with her, for no word of a lie she was the finest jewel there!

When he was gone Cú Chulainn got sorry and followed Cú Rí out explaining the position, that she was his girl like. Well, Cú Rí Mac Dáire got into a tearing temper—that's one thing that will vex a Kerryman, try and take his woman off him! He was holding Bláthnaid with one hand for she was kicking like the devil. With his free hand he took Cú Chulainn by the two lapels of the coat and lifting him high above his head he sunk him into the soft ground up to the oxters, and putting his hand into a soft platter of cow dung he rubbed it into Cú Chulainn's face. Made off with Bláthnaid and never drew halt till he landed at Cathair Con Rí in Kerry where his stronghold was, but Bláthnaid refused to have anything to do with him. She ran upstairs and locked herself into the top room and if he shook gold under her feet she wouldn't come down to him.

Well, when Cú Chulainn was dug up in the morning, I tell you it was hard to shave him. He collected his men together and they went tearing through Ireland in search of the King of Kerry. As he was in disguise they didn't know where to look for him, but they kept going. One day they were camped down near Castlegregory. Cú Chulainn told 'em take it easy for the day and taking his rod he went fishing. He walked on by the banks of the river Finglas until it became a stream and without knowing it where was he standing but under Cú Rí Mac Dáire's stronghold. He saw someone waving to him from a top window and when it turned out to be Bláthnaid, he waved back and they carried on a conversation in sign language, and she told him 'twas no good to try and take the stronghold now. He'd have to wait until the stream below would turn to white.

Bláthnaid then went down to Cú Rí and was as nice as pie to him. Even hinted that it might be all right now about the marriage. That pleased the King of Kerry and he wanted to know when the big day would be. 'Not,' says she, 'until you put up a new palace, for this is only a pokeen of a place and nothing like what I was used to in the Isle of Man.'

So Cú Rí called together every able bodied man in his kingdom, and a fine show they made every man as tall as his king and built according.

He then dispatched his men to the four corners of Ireland to bring back the biggest slabs of stone and the finest trees of timber to build the new palace. When they were gone Bláthnaid was making talk with the king and she said half joking half in earnest wasn't it a great wonder he wouldn't wash himself.

Now that man no more needed washing than I do myself. This was a blind as we'll see. As the royalty of that time wouldn't be seen dead inside in water, whatever servants were there filled a big tank with milk. Cú Rí peeled off and went into it, gave himself a thorough washing. She was waiting with towels when he came out, and as he was drying himself he sat with his back to this pillar with the sun shining down on him. Bláthnaid began to comb his hair that was never cut since he was born, and with the rack she ran a crease back through the centre of his crown and combed the hair out on the two sides. Then she plaited it into two enormous tails and pretending to have fun she brought the tails around the pillar and put a knot at the back. His hands couldn't reach around to the knot; he was a prisoner. She ran up then and pulled the plug out of the tank and the milk ran down into the river. This was the signal for Cú Chulainn to come charging into the fortress and it is said that as they came at him this mighty man killed fifty of them with his hands and fifty with his feet, and as he died he gave vent to a great cry that was heard in the four corners of Ireland, and the Kerrymen hearing it. . . every man that had a slab of stone on his shoulder pitched it point first into the ground and every man that had a tree of timber threw it from him—and this accounts for the gulane stones you see standing up and down the country and the *creachaills* of bog dale when turf is cut to the stone.

The Kerrymen rushed into the fort but before they had time to get their swords Cú Chulainn's warriors swarmed on top of them and left, right and centre they laid them low—gutted 'em. There was no respect for human life then. Bláthnaid was there and calling out she said, 'There's one man must not be killed and that's Fergus the bard, he knows where Cú Rí's gold is hidden.'

Fergus said he'd show Bláthnaid the cave where the treasure was, and leading her to the edge of the cliff, he threw open his cloak and putting his arms around her and shouting, 'Revenge for Cú Rí' he plunged with her over the brink, and down they fell and the loose rocks and the shale crashed down after 'em and buried 'em below!

Cú Chulainn had to go home without wife or fortune and the women of Kerry cursed him and he going, for he left them without husbands or sweethearts. But they weren't long idle. Whatever single men were in Cork came in and married them, which accounts for the fact down to this present day whenever the two counties are playing football you'll hear the shout from the Kerry sideline, 'Shove into 'em, boy, and remember your mother's people!'

CHAPTER EIGHT

MICK THE FIDDLER COMES HOME

There were also those who came back from America—those who only went over to see the time. Such a man was Mick the Fiddler. He said the climate over didn't agree with him. He got a crick in his neck from looking up at the tall buildings.

The day before he sailed for America Mick helped his brother and his brother's wife Moll Phil to set the barley in the high field—he was home again in time to cut it! His brother went to the Railway Station to meet him, and when Mick the Fiddler got off the sidecar above at the gable of his own house, he looked around at the countryside and said: 'So this is Ireland!' Only gone six months! He had a crease in his trousers that'd shave a gooseberry for you, and the tie he had around his neck I wouldn't like any bull to see it! He didn't know anyone that came to meet him, even those who were in the same book as him going to school. He went straight into the kitchen, and very taken aback by the way at what he saw sitting up on the hob by the fire. He said to his brother's wife:

'Say, Moll, what's this longtailed bugger in the corner?'

'Wisha, Mick,' says she, 'is it how you don't know the cat!'

But of all the people ever to come back from America, Mick the Fiddler gave the best of value, for he answered all questions appertaining to the nature of New York. Signs by, the house used to be packed every night and the brother and the brother's wife, Moll Phil, pusses on 'em, for they usedn't get to bed until all hours. Another thing, Moll Phil was very house-proud. Her kitchen was shining. You could eat off the floor, and it killed her to see all of us streaming in every night, bringing the mud of the locality on our shoes.

Mick's first night home he was telling us about the boat going over. He said they must have saved the company a fortune on food. It was four days before they could keep anything down. In those days all emigrant boats had to pull in to Ellis Island in New York Harbour, where they had to undergo a very strict medical examination.

A newspaper would be held up in front of you, and you'd be expected to read a skein out of it. They were all good scholars going over that time, but again there might be the occasional man that wouldn't know B from a bull's foot up on the gable of a house. He'd be questioned to see how the talk was by him. He'd be asked what is a cloud? Or to explain a mountain. Mick said one of the Hanna Finns up there near Loo Bridge made an awful bad fist of the reading. Poor fellow, I suppose he got excited, so the American said to him: 'Say, can you tell me what a lake is?'

Finn said: 'I can and will tell you what a lake is. 'Tis a hole in the arse of a kettle!'

Mick told us when it came to the medical examination you'd be prodded and poked the same as if you were a bullock at the fair. The way the doctor'd look through the hair of your head and under your finger nails, you wouldn't be one bit surprised if he looked up a certain place to see was your backbone straight!

All the clothes, Mick said, had to be taken off, even the socks, and put in a little *cábúis* and you walked in naked to the doctor. When Mick was walking in naked, who should he meet charging out against him but one of the Casey's of Túirneóin-neach make a fig leaf with two hands. '*Fo fó thiona,*' says he, mad with fright, 'where's my trousers, 'tis a lady doctor that's inside!' The Caseys were ever virtuous! Mick said he'd be better off if he covered his face instead. She mightn't know him when he went in again!

Mick's first job over was working in a shoe store where a beautiful lady came in one day for a pair of shoes. Like many beautiful women, according to Mick, she had one small fault—she had an awful big *spág* of a foot. And nothing'd satisfy that girl, Mick said, only the fanciest pair of shoes in the house, and of course the shoes refused to go on her. Mick was trying to be of all the help he could. She'd find it hard to get a more attentive assitant. Down with him on one knee, and in an effort to get her heel into the shoe, he took the liberty of taking her by the leg. Looking down at him she said, 'Have you a horn?'

Mick's next job was drawing water in a big barrel in a four-horse car for baptising black and white babies. They weren't piebald, Mick told us, a handful black and a handful white. At this time it seems the population of New York was mounting. In the chapel where Mick was working there were four curates, their sleeves folded up to their elbows,

60

baptising away all day and the water flowing out the front door.

The same as here, those babies were baptised in the bottom of the church, but wakes were held in a funeral parlour. Mick was at one of these wakes. He told us the man was laid out in a coffin with the lid off, and he dressed up in a new suit—no habit—the same as if he was going to a dance. Mick thought it a shame burying the new suit with him, until someone called him aside and told him there was no back to the suit! I tell you, the Yanks'd learn you how to live!

The wake he was at. . . he was a Dannehy boy from the butt of the Paps. He fell under a train at Penn. Station. Mick took the day off to go to the wake, and on the way he called into a Speakeasy, it was during prohibition, where he struck up a friendship with an American born Kerryman. They used to call those narrabacks, so the two set out for the wake. The narraback didn't know Dannehy or the sky over him, but he said he'd go along for the fun of it. They called to a few more saloons on the way and when they arrived they were spifflicated, paralytic, and missed the funeral parlour by inches. They went in next door knelt down and mustering up all the reverence they could, they began to pray. Where were they kneeling but in front of a piano with a lid up. Luck of God, they didn't put their elbows on the bed. They got up and walking away the narraback said to Mick: 'I did not have the privilege of knowing your friend, but I must say he sure had a fine set of teeth!'

I'll never forget as long as I live one night we were in the house and Mick the Fiddler was on his favourite subject—skyscrapers. There was a man there that had been on an excursion to Cork, and he said: 'Well now, Mick, would those skyscrapers be as tall as one of the spires of St Finbarr's Cathedral in Cork?' Mick looked at him. 'God help your head! They'd go down that far in New York before they'd even think of going up! And they go up so high they had to take a brick off one chimney to let the moon pass!'

And those buildings go up so quick. Mick said he was going to work one morning. They were digging out the foundations for a new skyscraper, and when he was coming home from work that evening the tenants were being evicted for non-payment of rent. That put the Round Towers and the Gobán Saor in the ha'penny place!

There were so many questions to Mick about the topography of New York that he decided he'd draw a map. There was no piece of paper in the house big enough so what did Mick do only put a coating of ashes on the flag of the fire, and with the top of old Din Donovan's walking cane he drew in the ashes the outline of the island of Manhattan. Ten miles long, Mick said, and three miles wide, bought by the Dutch from the Red Indians for less than fifty dollars. 'Don't you think,' says Mick, 'there were bargains going in those days!'

With the top of Din Donovan's walking cane he drew the avenues running north and south and the streets running across, and he said the number of buildings between two streets was called a block, and that there were eight blocks to the mile—if you could believe him. He began to show us places. The names were as well known to us as the townlands of our own parish. The Bowery and Chinatown, and he said there was a Kenmare Street in Chinatown—weren't they caught short for names! Riverside Drive, Hell's Kitchen, Columbus' Circle and Central Park West. Well, there a simple poor man there and looking at the map he said, 'I'd know where in the middle of all that ashes is my sister Hanna?' 'Do you know her number?' says Mick. 'Two hundred and forty West Eighty Fourth Street.' 'Right,' says Mick pointing down with the walking cane, 'between Amsterdam and Broadway. There is where she hangs out!' Which was true for him for she worked in a laundry.

The cat sat up on the hob and began to wash her front, then arching her back she opened her mouth wide—you'd swear she was laughing. The dog was lying on the floor a bit down from the fire. If he only knew half of him was inside in the Hudson. There he was with his snout down on his two front paws a few inches away from the ashes of Mick's map. He was barking in his sleep, and isn't it lovely to hear him 'wuff, wuff, wuff', whatever little images are running through his mind. I suppose that he pictures himself after sheep on the mountain, or maybe mixed up in some other carry on!

The dog took a deep breath, filled himself up, you could nearly count his ribs. Then of a sudden he let it all down his nose in one snort and demolished three-quarters of an acre of skyscrapers! You could see the little particles of ashes rising up between you and the light of the lamp, and you could see Moll Phil's face, and it was like the map of South America!

Well, there were Breshnihins there who had brothers in the Bronx, Sheehans who had sisters in Staten Island and Keoghs who had cousins in Queens, not to mind those with relations in Brooklyn, Yonkers and the Jersey Shore. 'Twas like a pantomime they all wanting to know where their people were living. But Mick told 'em, as all these places were outside the island of Manhattan—up the Hudson and down the bay turn to Coney and Rockaway—the chairs had to be pulled back and more ashes brought out to add to the map!

In the middle of all this activity the cat hopped off the hob and marched down Fifth Avenue— you'd think it was Patrick's Day. We began to call the cat in case she'd bring the ashes on her pads all over the house. And the dog woke up when he heard us talking to the cat, thinking he was being left out of something. Got up and walked over and sat down in the middle of the Bronx and began to wag his tail. Now the ashes began to rise and Mick the Fiddler knew the fat was in the fire so he started to call the dog. Cess! Cess! Cess! Nice doggie. Nice doggie! And the dog, a big soft, half fool of a sheep-dog, to show his friendship sent his tail around like a propeller churning up the ashes until you couldn't see your finger in front of your face. Out of this dense fog came Moll Phil with the sweeping brush, and as I was the nearest to her I got the first crack of it. 'Aha,' says she, 'I'll give ye the Bronx! And I'll give ye Chinatown!' The same as if she was the mounted police, she cleared the kitchen. We all spilled out the front door like dirty water out of a bucket, bringing to an abrupt ending Mick the Fiddler's graphic description of the island of Manhattan in the State of New York in the Continent of America. They went the low road, I came the high road, they crossed by the stepping stones, I came over the bridge, they were drowned and I was saved, and all I ever got out of my story telling was shoes of brown paper and stockings of thick milk. *Níl agam ach a chuala níor chuala ach a duaradh agus ní duaradh fairíor ach bréaga.* (I only know what I heard I only heard what was said and what was said I am afraid was lies!)

CHAPTER NINE

KILLING THE PIG

Mick the Fiddler, like all the returned yanks, when he wore out the clothes he came home in, you wouldn't know him from the man that never stirred out. He sat at my father's fire when his day's work was over, and talked with the other men about the life around us, and the things that mattered most in that life, food, drink and tobaccy, love, marriage and the hereafter!

Oh God on High that rules the sky come in
    the open door.
And bring us mate that we can ate
    and take away the boar!

That was the prayer of a servant, when his master killed a very old gentleman pig! Why then when I was young it'd be the poor man that'd let the winter past without killing a pig. And if you went into a house in November, you'd have to pick your way to keep from banging your head into the flitches of bacon hanging down from the rafters smoking away!

Not everyone could cure a pig. Some'd overdo the salt, others'd be too skimpy with it—you'd hear of those that'd put a dust of brown sugar or a pinch of saltpetre in it for flavouring. No matter!

If it was done right 'twas hard to cap the home cured bacon. Say what you like, *a mhico*, there was no better dish for the working man.

And wasn't the fresh pork lovely! And the puddings! Oh my! When we were nippers we'd give our two eyes out for the puddings! Puttens we used to call 'em. So there's no harm in saying that it was an event in the house the day the pig was killed.

Although women had no heart for the slaughter: the women in this house, used to take to the fields, their fingers in their ears, for the screeching of a stuck pig would curdle the blood! As a child I used to be a bit terrified myself. Of course, I used get very fond of the pig while he was fattening. No day'd pass that I wouldn't give him a call. I found the most agreeable time to visit him in his *Árus*, was when his belly was full. He'd often sit on his behind—his head to one side looking at me with his small eyes as he scratched his waistcoat with one of the two toes of his hind leg. He'd always take it as a great favour if I gave a rub of my heel to a place he couldn't get at, and the fatter he got the more places got out of reach.

Passing neighbours'd be brought to have a look at him by my mother. They'd marvel at how he had improved since the last time. You'd think the pig'd be enjoying all this admiration, until he'd get a slap of a hat on the rump to make him walk around, so that the neighbours could guess his weight and compliment my mother on his condition. Poor fellow, if he only knew, every extra pound he put on brought the day nearer when he'd wind up in the pot.

Green grew the rushes o,
   the blackbird and the thrushes o,
We'll kill the pig with the curly tail,
   and we'll have mate tomorr-ee-o.

For the purpose of killing the pig there was in every locality an expert butcher, and the man we had there, credit where credit is due, was quick to dispatch! From the time the pig found himself on the flat of his back on the table in the yard, four men steadying him for the knife, until he was hanging by the hind legs from the ladder, scalded, shaved and emptied out, with three pointed sally rods keeping his waistcoat open, and a big spud in his mouth, everyone worked like lightening and it was all over in a flash.

A few of the neighbours'd be in again the following night for the salting. And how many stone of salt'd cure a pig? I'm told three stone is overdoing it. Two and a half stone is enough! Well I should know it! Many is the time I brought it across the handlebars of the bike from Barraduff!

We used to nail a board around the table to keep the salt from falling on the floor. The salt was rubbed well into the flesh with the fingers and the palm of the hand, and deep pockets'd be made for it to carry the brine to the bone. And when the last piece'd be put in position in the big tub—a wine barrel we'd use—and a weighty *carraig* put on top of it to press it down, the man of the house'd be happy. But of course his worries wouldn't be over till the ninth day when the pickle'd be expected to rise. If it didn't rise'd be a calamity, but if it did, it'd keep rising, and in three weeks' time it'd be up to the top, and your bacon was cured only to hang it up. And once there was york in the garden, swedes in the haggard and spuds in the pit no one in that house'd be hungry for the winter.

But to come back to the puddings! Here is where the women shone. From early morning the day after killing the pig, they'd be down to the river turning what seemed to be miles of intestines inside out and washing 'em in the running stream.

In the house then, in a while's time, they'd be all around this big pot, where they were after mixing Macroom oatenmeal and milk with the pig's blood, added to that'd be rice, onions, breadcrumbs, pepper, salt, all spice and the diggle knows what else.

Then the intestines'd be cut into lengths of up to eighteen inches. One end would be tied with a bit of bageen thread, and the lovely way the women had of keeping the other end open like a funnel with the thumb and first finger of the left hand, and then with the free hand they'd begin ladling in the mixture with a big spoon—and the filling of the puddings was in full swing!

When a pudding was three quarters full—room had to be left for expansion in the cooking—the ends'd be tied together to make a bowlie, it looked for all the world like a small bicycle tube pumped up. Then over the fire'd be another big pot, the handle of a brush across the mouth of it, and the women'd run these hanks of pudding in over the handle of the brush, in a form that the greater bulk of the puddings'd be dipping into the boiling water. Then they'd be turned around as they cooked getting an occasional prod of the fork to keep 'em from bursting. When they'd be all done there'd be a string of puddings from here down to the dresser, and take it or lave it, there wouldn't be one of 'em

69

left two mornings after. For at that time the custom was when you had the plenty you'd share it with your neighbour and he'd do the same with you when God smiled on him! A plate of pork steak a finger high, and a circle of pudding, maybe two, would find its way to every house in the townland. What a heart the people had then, and if you or me were to put our foot inside the door of any of those houses when that pork or pudding was sizzling in the pan, you'd be invited to sit over to the table and share it. Though it would not be thought proper manners or good rearing to be in a hurry accepting it. 'No, no, no,' you'd say I only left the table after me!

That was the old way and a person that'd take food or drink in a neighbour's house, or even sing a song at a dance, without a little forcing, was considered forward!

I had an uncle living at the other side of the mountain, and one morning long before I was confirmed I was sent over to my uncle's to know would himself and Mary come over to us when we were having the stations. I was over the mountain once with my father so I thought I knew the way.

After a while climbing I wasn't so sure for nowhere could I see the little landmarks my father pointed out to me. I made poor headway on rough ground. Times I'd put my head over a knob thinking I was at the top, only to find that I had as far more to go. The day was going and the hunger began to pick me, but I kept going and when I got to the top of the mountain the heart was put across me altogether for the fog fell.

'Don't move in the fog—wait until it lifts,' my father'd say. So I sat down, but the quietness and the queer things I thought I saw in the drifting fog made me afraid, so I began to aise myself with the fall, feeling with my feet and holding on to the heather with my hands, until after ages I heard a small sound of water tinkling. I knew now, that I had covered a fair bit of ground, so I kept the little stream company till it brought me out of the fog. And there far below me I could see a house.

Was I divarted! With no bite gone inside my lips since morning the sight of a house was welcome. I belted down the side of the mountain and by the time I got into the yard it was dark. There was a light in the stall. A man came out and I asked him where was Íochtarchúil—where my uncle was living.

'Íochtarchúil,' says he, 'is away to the west of us. But no one in his proper senses would venture that far tonight. Come in and stay with us and I'll point out the way to you in the morning.'

I went in with him, and like the story while ago, I was born the right time for the table was being laid. It seems the old man and the son were at the fair that day, and it was only now they were having the dinner — Wasn't I in luck! The son's wife was there, a returned yank very likely, judging by the speech and the complexion.

The spuds were taken up, strained and put steaming. In a while's time they were turned out on the table and plates full of home cured bacon and cabbage. Oh Glory, and I ravenous! Then the woman of the house, give her her due, invited me to sit over, and of course I knowing my manners said—and you'd say it without thinking!

'No! No! No! Look if it killed me I couldn't touch it—I only left the table after me.'

She didn't ask me anymore! The old man and the son began to force me. She shut 'em up saying, 'Didn't you hear what the kid said!' And wasn't that the tantalising I got, to have to sit there looking at 'em stowing it away—the big mountain of spuds going down in the middle of the table and small mountains of peels rising at their elbows.

And then to kill me altogether. What did they do? Fed the dog, within a foot of me! I was going to say let me bring it out in the yard to him so that I could ate it myself. And I'd say he'd let me too for he was a friendly old buffer!

The table was cleared and we all sat up to the fire, and there, so near me, I could put my hand into it, was the pot nearly a quarter full of potatoes. I was praying that nature'd call 'em out, but it didn't, or if it did it didn't call 'em out together!

Bedtime came and I was put down in the room with the old man. There were two fine camp beds below. Well, I thought he'd never doze off. He was so curious! He wanted to know every single thing about everyone belonging to me, but when he found out I wasn't related to anyone important he began to yawn and fell asleep.

I waited till his snoring was nice and regular, and then I crept out of the bed doing my level best to avoid the chair where my clothes were draped. It was as dark as pitch. I tried opening the door and one of the hinges began to complain. I put my weight on the latch. That worked, and I was in the kitchen. Not knowing what I'd bump into there, I thought it safer to go down on all fours and crawl.

After a time I made an attempt to rise and got an unmerciful wallop on the top of the head. Where was I, you diggle, but under the table, and

72

not alone there for something cold and wet tipped me in the face. I'd have passed out then, only for thinking of the dog. It could be worse if he barked!

From where I was now, I could make out the hearth, so I crept up feeling for the pot. I found it, and with no implements no more than Adam had, I settled in to ate the spuds. I don't remember enjoying any Christmas dinner like it.

When I was full I walked down, my eyes getting used to the dark now, and using the same trick of putting my weight on the latch, I shut the room door without making a sound.

But this time I suppose I was getting too cock sure of myself, for, I fell over the chair and woke up the old man!

He cracked a match and when he saw me standing there in my shirt he pointed under the bed, saying:

'You didn't have to go out at all then, perishing yourself!'

I didn't say anything only hopped into bed and dropped off. When I got up in the morning the woman of the house was making a great sing song about the empty pot of spuds.

'Where,' says she, 'could they have gone to?'

'Yerra, I suppose,' her husband said, 'the dog ate 'em!'

'Why then if he did,' she said, 'in the circus he should be, for he peeled 'em as well.'

CHAPTER TEN

AFTER HOURS

Well, there was this public house I knew of a time. You'd hardly ever see anyone going into it or coming out of it. It was run by three sisters, fairly ancient, I'd say they were behind the door when the good looks were being given out. You'd want to be paid if you were to give any time looking at 'em. One of the sisters'd always be at the entrance, dyddling away for herself, looking up and down the street, the two hands under the apron. By the way, do you see, that it was a gay house.

The time the railways and the roads were cut during the second trouble there was an awful shortage of drink in town, and Ned Connor, when all fruit fails welcome haws, went into the public house I'm talking about. Ned had an awful mind for porter, he'd drink it out of a horse's crupper. The sister that was at the door dyddling the blackbird backed in before him.

Ned called for a pint, and when after a lot of *taoscing* she put it on the counter, Ned said,

'This pint isn't full.'

'Ah,' says she, 'I left room on top for your moustache.'

Ned had what can only be described as a big straggly growth on the top lip. When he put up the money she found she was a few ha'pence short. The price of the moustache Ned told her. The porter was so flat, little *súilíns* winking on top of it, that it gave Ned enough to do to finish the pint.

When finally he got it down Ned made a move to go, and as she dyddled she kept an eye on him.

'Are you off?' she said.

'Oh I am,' says Ned.

'Of course,' says she, turning as sour as the commodity she was selling, 'only for the shortage of drink in town you wouldn't come into me at all.'

'Well I can tell you one thing,' says Ned, 'you'll have a lot of dyddling done before I'll come into you again!'

Ned was noted, but fierce, for the drink. He took every known pledge in his time including the anti-treating pledge. That was brought in to counteract the habit of standing your round, which is all right if the company is small, but if you have seven or eight in a batch, and maybe, before you know where you are, the man that opened the proceedings is off on the second leg of the course, then there's rough weather ahead. And the man of limited capacity don't he suffer! His wife at home thinking he is enjoying himself.

One of the pledges Ned took only allowed him one drink a day. He settled for a pint. That was all right until he was seen pouring two pints into a quart jug, making one drink of it. He went from the quart to the sweet gallon and finished up worse than ever. And I'll never forget one Whitsun I was going doing the rounds at Gobnet's Well, John Lynch was with me the same day and we got up to Ned going down Sliabh Riabhach.

Whit was late that year and it was very warm so

we went into The Mills. I called and when the pints were put on the counter Ned Connor caught his glass and ran out in the yard with it. When he came back t'was empty. John Lynch called then, and the same thing happened. Ned came back with the empty glass in his hand. T'was his own turn to call then and when he was making for the back door with the third pint t'was only natural that myself or John Lunch'd remark on it. Well, for one thing he was playing poo-paw with the conversation, so I said—'*Croí an diabhail*, Ned where are you going with the pints or what class of caper is this?'

'Ah lads,' says he, 'have patience with me I have a pledge against drinking in public houses.' Of course as the day wore on he forgot to go out and broke that pledge too!

Ned was married. God help the poor children they were often hungry and the wife was to be pitied. Now it so happened that the wife had an aunt. A pure druidess of a one. She came visiting and she wasn't long in the house when she pointed out to Ned the error of his ways. He had to go down on his knees and promise that he'd give the drink the go-by or she said she'd make a *lúbán* of him, and she would, for she was a fierce major of a woman. She marched him into the convent to Sister Binidict and made him take the teetotaller's pledge.

And to everyone's surprise he kept it—well for a while. One day in town he fell into bad company and broke out. He arrived home paralatic. He had to hold on to the back of a chair in an effort to maintain his relationship with the perpendicular and to make things worse his wife's aunt was there. Did she read him a lesson!

'After all the promises you made,' says she. 'A man with such little respect for his word, not to mind the welfare of his wife and family, could not expect to see the light of heaven! A nice husband! and a nice father. Have you no fear of the hereafter? And what would you do if the Lord called on you this minute.'

'To tell you the truth, auntie,' says Ned. 'I couldn't stir a leg!'

Ned went steady after that—he had to for the wife's aunt came to live in the house with 'em, but even in time she relented a small bit. Ned was allowed to go back to one of his former pledges, a pint a day—no quarts or sweet gallons—just, as the aunt put it, one imperial pint a day. Ned got into the habit of taking the pint about closing time or a little after it, and there is a bit of history attached to that too, and I might as well tell it while I'm at it.

Ned had a white tom cat that used folly him everywhere. He'd go up the stairs after him every night when he was going to bed. Ned'd be tricking with him and they'd have a little boxing match through the banisters of the stairs. When Ned'd take his trousers off and put it on the seat of the chair, the cat'd make a hammock of that until morning. He'd cross the street every night after him and sit on the window-sill of the pub until Ned came out.

The cat was as well known as a bad ha'penny. People passing along the village at night and seeing him sitting on the window-sill of Meskill's pub knew that Ned Connor was inside having his daily imperial, which he never went beyond and his temperance brought him a little prosperity. You see he had a fine roomy house and the wife encouraged by the aunt began to keep people—turned it into an aiting house.

Two young guards used to have their dinner there. The force was only in its infancy at the time. The guards weren't long coming to the house when they were like one of the family. Yerra, they'd go in and sit in the kitchen, and throw their caps on top of the dresser. In the kitchen they came to know the cat. They came to know too about Ned's habit of going across the road to Meskill's for his daily pint after closing time, and knowing Ned so well they'd never raid the pub while the cat was sitting outside on the window-sill.

Raiding pubs was almost a nightly occurance that time, for the licensing laws were not as liberal then as they are now. The weekly paper'd be full of court cases. I saw it given down myself where a guard at twelve o'clock at night after being given an assurance by the publican that there was no one on the premises, went upstairs, opened the door of a wardrobe and a man fell out. People'd go into an auger hole rather than have their names in the paper!

The guard swore that in another room he found three men sound asleep in a small bed with the clothes up to their chins, the picture of innocence. What they didn't know was that their feet were cocking out at the bottom.

'A wonder they didn't feel the cold!' says the Judge.

'How could they,' said the guard, 'and they having their shoes on!'

But to go back to Ned. I was in Meskills myself one night when he came in. Even though it was gone closing time there was a big crowd inside. There was something on in the village the same day.

78

I think it was a bull inspection. The publican was in no hurry out with 'em and now that Ned was in, and the cat outside he felt safe. . . at least for the length of time it took Ned to down one imperial pint.

The talk was nice an' leisurely and Ned'd be no more than half way down the glass when there was a sharp knock at the front door.

'Open up in the name of the law!'

'*Croi an diabhail*,' says Ned, 'it must be strange guards. Our own lads'd have noticed the cat!'

'Clear,' says the publican, frightened of an endorsement, 'out the back!' as he began to pour drink down the shore. In another second the lights were out, total eclipse, and there was what I can only describe as a stampede towards where we thought the back door should be. We were going into presses and everything. And when we found the door the first of the crowd out were bolting back like a squad of rabbits that'd meet a ferrit in the turn of a burrow! There was another guard at the back gate!

Now, we made for the stairs, and some of us got out the upper window on to the roof of a shed, and the plan was, if our geography was correct, to get down into a neighbour's yard and make good our escape. And do you know what I'm going to say! The corrugated iron roof of a shed on a wet night is an awful slippery place. The legs were taken from under one fellow and he went sliding down and fell ten feet on top of God only knows what! I could not repeat here what he said, and he had hardly himself straightened when another fellow fell on top of him.

Well, there was one huge corporation of a man

there—they told me after he was home from South Africa on holidays—and we were all hanging out of him. Blessed hour tonight if the man didn't lose his balance, and crashed on the flat of his back on the roof bringing us all down with him. Such a report! Cows, pigs, geese, all the animals in the vicinity woke up, as we went skeeting down the roof and fell on top of one another into the black hole of Calcutta!

Then you heard the language! Drink lubricates the talking machine—'twas like Dunkirk! And to make matters worse, whatever way it happened, down into the publican's yard we fell. The guards were there before us, our names were taken, so we had all our work for nothing!

When we came out in the street Ned Connor went straight to the window-sill, but there was no sign of the white cat. He couldn't believe his eyes. Whatever look we gave, there below on the school wall was Ned Connor's white cat holding a loud conversation with a member of his own community, and she seemed to be saying to him 'Not now-ow-ow. Not now-ow-ow.'

'Well bad manners to you anyway, Pangur Bán!' says Ned rubbing his shins, 'I'd have nearly gone without my imperial pint tonight if I knew you had a date!'

CHAPTER ELEVEN

TOBACCO

There was a man here near us, a cobbler, and he was full sure that John Bull was a certain rich man living in a big mansion over in London. And when the old age pension came out in 1908, nothing in the world 'd convince him, but that John Bull was paying it all out of his own pocket! The cobbler was going around saying, 'He must be rotten with money and all of it he's giving away!'

But to go back to 1908. One comical result of the news that a pension was coming in for everyone over seventy was, that some women aged ten years in one night!

One woman, we all heard of, whenever she'd have a row with the husband she'd grig him with— 'The fooleen I was, a young girl like me, to marry an old lad like you, ten years older than me. Wasting my life on you!' As it turned out she was drawing the pension before him. Or can anyone believe daylight from women! They were quick to take the pension!

But joking apart, it is very hard for us to realise how badly off old people were at that time. You see, they'd have given over their house and land to a son. Of course there used to be an agreement or an understanding that the old couple would remain on in the place and be supported. In return for that support the old man 'd work in the fields as long as he was able, and the old woman 'd give a hand around the house and mind the children as long as she was able.

Old people could be an asset in the house, and the generations could get along fine together and they did. The one fly, of course, in the ointment, could be the son's wife. A lot depended on her and on her nature. She'd have her own young children to occupy her and as the old people got older and more helpless they might be coming in her way, and relations, as the man said, could get strained! They'd be strangers in her eyes and if she was hard-hearted she'd begrudge 'em the very bite that went into their mouths.

In one house, not a thousand miles from where I'm sitting, they had a bull in the tub; at dinner time the daughter-in-law put a bit of beef the size of a half-a-crown in the old man's plate. God, it looked miserable alongside a mountain of turnips. He called for more. She gave him another bit of beef the size of a shilling and a big scoop of turnips.

'Gi' me more mate!' says he.

'You've enough,' she told him. 'If you ate any more of it the bull'll be roaring inside you.'

'Why then,' says he, 'it won't be for the want of turnips!'

I tell you the pension was a blessing to old people. It made 'em independent, although it was only five shillings in 1908, or maybe only half-a-crown. They were able to contribute towards their support, and the man could invest in a half-quarter of tobaccy, and the woman in an ounce of snuff, if she was that way inclined. Bonar Law or Asquith, or whoever brought in that pension, should be given a medal—there are statues being put up to men that did nothing!

Prior to the pension there was this old man, and like the story a while ago, he was living with his son and daughter-in-law. They had a rising family and because of that, and the poverty of the times and the poorness of the land, they were pulling the devil by the tail. But the daughter-in-law was a big-hearted woman, a good servant, and whatever was going, everyone, including the old man, got his fair share. But she drew the line at that. Not one ha' penny would she spend on tobaccy for him.

And I wouldn't mind but he was a martyr to the pipe. He'd give his right hand from the elbow down, for a smoke. Usedn't he try and cure the leaves of the *cupóg* and smoke it—he used! And he'd smoke white turf. Some brands of that were very hot. He'd have to lie on the bed after with his tongue out trying to cool it!

His eyes used to get watery for the want of a smoke. He'd get so blind walking along the road, he'd be saluting gate piers.

'That you John! Have you any bit of tobaccy!'

Even the bush growing out of the side of the ditch, he'd think it was a saddle horse! *An buile tobac* the old people'd call that form of madness.

The time I'm talking about his eldest grandson was about seven or eight years. He and his grandfather were great friends; they were as thick as a cow and cock of hay. And it used to grieve the little *garsún* to see his granda suffering for the want of a smoke. Often when the two of 'em would be sitting down together minding the cows out of the rhygrass the young lad'd say:

83

'Granda! Granda! When I'm big I'm going to get an awful lot of money and what am I going to buy for you?'

'An ounce of tobaccy.' the old man 'd say. 'You can keep the rest of it for yourself!'

And short as the legs were under the grandson, you'd often see him belting across the fields if he heard a neighbour was at a wake or a funeral, to know would he have even half a pipeful of tobaccy for his granda.

If ever he succeeded in getting a knob of plug, he'd call his granda behind the car-house where there was a seat in the *cúl gháirdín*, and sitting there together he'd watch the old man cut up the tobaccy, and then break it with his fingers into *brúscar* in the palm of his left hand, very careful not to let the smallest morsel of it fall on the ground.

Then there'd be a big ceremony preparing the pipe, scraping the inside of it with the knife and turning the ashes into the pipe cover, which 'd be made out of a blackening tin. A few handy taps with the handle of the knife on the bottom of the upturned pipe to make sure it was empty. Then he'd put it in his mouth and suck the air through it. A thousand pounds to a penny it would be blocked, so the young lad'd have to go and get a *tráithnín* to act as a *réiteoir*.

He'd watch his granda take the pipe apart at the place where the silvery ferrule was, and run the *tráithnín* through the short stem until it disappeared, and when it came out the other side the fox's tail at the end of the sop'd be as black as the ace of spades—the same as if you pulled a bush through a chimney.

Then, after freeing that part of the stem from

the ferrule up to the head, his granda 'd put the pipe together, put it in his mouth, and this time you could hear air whistling through it. Now, to fill it. The mouth of the pipe'd be put under the palm of the left hand, and with the right fore-finger his granda'd coax the tobaccy into the pipe, searching the crevices of his palm and in between his fingers for any stray particles of the precious weed. Then the ashes in the cover'd be spread on top and pressed down, not too hard, with the thumb. Nothing now but to redden it!

He'd have no match of course! Only millionaires had matches that time, so he 'd cut a strong twig, bring it to a sharp point with the knife and give it to the grandson. He'd go into the kitchen and spear a half-red coal of fire and bring it out. The old man'd blow the coal to get a little flame. Then he'd put the coal on top of the pipe, maybe shading it with his hat, start to puff and in a few seconds he'd be going like a limekiln. But it would have to get nice and red before he'd put on the cover, and then he was smoking in earnest.

A great look of contentment'd come over his face and the *garsún*'d smile to see his oul gran' so happy. After the smoke the old man'd be in form to sing a bit of a song, a quiet *crónán*.

If all the fair maidens were hares
    on the mountain,
Very soon the young men'd get guns
    and go fowling.
Tah ral dah ral die do ral rex tee ding tol die day.

If all the fair maidens were blackbirds
    and thrushes,
Very soon the young men'd be baiting

the bushes.

Tah ral dah ral die do ral, rex tee ding fol die day.

If all the fair maidens were green rushes growing,
Very soon the young men'd get scythes
   and go mowing.

Tah ral, dah ral die do ral, rex tee ding fol die day.

I don't think people lived as long that time as
they do now. Anyway it came to the old man's
turn, and he was called away. The children were
put up to bed in the loft earlier than usual that
evening. The house had to be readied, and provisions got for neighbours and relatives that'd be
coming to the wake.

Sometime out in the night the grandson woke
up. He thought it strange all that buzz of conversation under him. Then he remembered. It must be
the wake. He never saw a wake before. He stole out
of the bed and over to the well of the stairs. The
kitchen was full. Some people were sitting over to
the table drinking tae, a thing he wouldn't get himself only once in a wonder. There was no shortage.
Little did the child know that people used to break
themselves that time in order to have a good wake.

He could see saucers of snuff going around.
Everyone taking a pinch and praying:

'The Lord have mercy on his soul.'

'Solus na bhflaitheas dúinn go léir.'

'Amen, *a Thiarna*!'

'He's in heaven anyway.'

'What did he ever do to anyone!'

'All his life trying to make ends meet!'

The next thing he saw was a man going around
with a bucket of porter and handing out cups of it.
And he said to himself, 'they all liked my granda!'

If he only knew, some of 'em hardly knew him.

The place was full of smoke. The child thought the chimney wasn't pulling. Not at all, 'twas tobaccy smoke. The surprise he got to see every man and some of the old women puffing away to their heart's content!

He came down the stairs and moving in and out through the crowd he made off to the room where his granda was laid out. 'Oh God help us poor oul gran. He got so small and so pale!'

The room was full of people too, and he couldn't take his eyes off two men that were there cutting tobaccy and filling it into clay pipes. And looking at all the tobaccy he ran over to the bed:

'Oh granda!' he said, 'isn't it an awful pity you didn't live till the stuff got plentyful.'

CHAPTER TWELVE

LOVE AND MARRIAGE

Haley was doing a line with one of the Cormacs. Two girls that were there living with the mother. Big mopseys they were too and very red in the complexions. There wasn't much humour in 'em. They were shy and awkward, very quiet, and would nearly burst out crying if you said goose to 'em.

Nonie was one of their names and I think the other one was called Delia. Oh *Dia linn*, what a family he picked! The mother was cute enough though, and when she heard who Nonie was doing the line with, she urged her to invite Haley into the kitchen. Bring it out in the open like, it mightn't be so easy for him then to back out of it. Anyway, Haley, was a good catch as we'll see farther on.

On the slope of the railway he used to be courting Nonie before that, but if the night turned wet they'd go into the car house. That was handy enough too, with a sop of straw under 'em in the body of the donkey car, though it was a devilish draughty place for there was no door to the front of it.

'Twas warmer in the kitchen. The only drawback there being the mother, and of course Delia. The mother would talk the hind leg off a duck. Conversation is all right if you haven't anything else in mind, and of course Haley had. After a few nights the mother took the hint. Nonie looking daggers at her, so she gathered herself down to bed.

The mother and the two daughters used to sleep in the room below the kitchen. But the devil a sleep the mother would go to until Haley was gone. She would too. The ear cocked. Haley as I said was a good match, a house to himself and a nice holding, so the mother was anxious to find out if he was serious as regards Nonie.

Anyway, it was common knowledge if he was going to marry it wouldn't be altogether out of blackguarding, for with no one in the house he wanted a woman. As we saw, the mother was gone down to bed, but still Haley didn't have Nonie to himself, for Delia was sitting there, two watery eyes on her, looking into the fire. After a while Haley got fed up of this, the night going, so he whispered to Nonie, and Nonie taking the hint gave Delia a nudge saying: 'Wouldn't you get up and go out and give a sop to the cows!'

Poor Delia got up and went out and stayed outside all night in the stall waiting for Haley to go. But when he got the house to himself the devil wouldn't shift him, the settle pulled over in front of the fire by the two of 'em. Haley liked his comfort. But if the silences were too long the mother below in the room would give a 'hm, hm!' and get a fit of coughing, so that for all the peace Haley got from that quarter he'd be as well off on the slope of the railway.

One night Delia was a bit late going out to throw a sop to the cows. She had a heavy pair of shoes on her, she was digging furrows the same day. And the mother below in the bed, hearing what sounded like a man's footsteps going out, and the clatter of the door closing she shouted up to the kitchen:

'Indeed and it was time for him to go. Come on down now the two of ye, and bring down the vessel before ye!'

Well, Nonie was mortified. Her complexion was always high, but she got as red as a turkey cock at the mother's remark. It had no effect on Haley. It would take more than that to embarrass that bucko.

After a year of the mother going to bed early every night, and poor Delia going out to throw a sop to the cows, Haley married Nonie. In Haley's house the wedding was, and people who were there told me it was a fine turn out. No expense spared, this and that there, currany tops and what-not, all kinds of grudles, buns, trifle and that shaky shivery stuff you'd ate with a spoon.

The wedding went on all night, into the following day as long as the drink held out! When all the 'goodbyes' were said, and all the relations gone, Haley and Nonie milked the cows and went to bed!

She was the first up in the morning, and she wasn't long at all gone downstairs to the kitchen when Haley heard her crying below. Down with him, and consoling her he said:

'Now, now, now, what's wrong with my little *circín*!'

'Oh,' says she, looking up the chimney. 'There's a loose flag above there in the flue, and when the little child comes to this house it'll fall down on him and kill him!'

'*Tanam an diúcs*!' says Haley getting over the shock at being introduced, so early on, to the contrariness that seems to strike women after marriage. The thought couldn't but cross his mind, that women were like little doves until you had 'em in the nest!

'Look now,' says he, all *grá mo chróí*, 'if it'll aise your mind at all, I'll mix a bit of mortar and I'll pin around the flag, and make it as firm as the rock of Gibealtar!'

A thing he did right away, though he was as black as a chimney sweep when it was over. A good job the little child hadn't come to the house. There'd be a hop knocked out of him when he saw the sort of father he had.

The day wore on, no other hitch and they went to bed again that night. She was first up in the morning, and she wasn't long below in the kitchen when he heard her crying again. Down with him and there was Nonie below striking her two hands together and kicking up an awful hullabulloo.

'What's wrong with you, crayther?' says he half shivering there in his shirt.

'Do you see those banisters there in the stairs?' says she. 'They are so near together that when the little child comes to this house he'll shove his head out between 'em and get choked!'

'If that's all the worry you have, 'tis soon rectified!' So he got a saw and cut out every second banister, saying 'By jamonies, he'll have to have an awful big head on him now to get caught between 'em!'

'He was praying that that'd be the end of it. *Mo léir cráite* she wasn't landed down in the kitchen the third morning, when he heard the *ologón*. He ran down and trying to control himself this time, he said:

'What's coming over you now?'

'Look at the cut of that yard,' says she, bringing

91

him over to the back door. 'And look at that big pool of *múnlach* in the middle of it, and when the little child comes to this house what's to prevent him from running down the pavings and falling into the *múnlach*, and getting drowned on me. And if you were a proper man and concerned about the feelings of your wife, you'd put the butt on the car and get a few loads of bog stuff and fill it up.'

'My patience,' says he, 'is worn to a thread, and don't think,' says he, 'that you're going to have me in a baitín boy running down the stairs every morning and listening to a cock and a bull story about what's going to happen to the little child when he comes to this house. If he's going to be anything like you, I can see that I have an exciting future ahead of me. I'm going away from you now,' says he, 'for I won't be consoled in my mind until I find out if there is another woman in the barony more contrary than the woman I married!'

And wouldn't you think it would be hard for him! He walked on, and in the course of his travels he met all varieties of women. Some of 'em beautiful, and as the man said, a beautiful woman is a jewel! Haley met these too, and he was beginning to think that if he was to keep his promise not to return home, until he met a woman more contrary than his wife, he'd never again see Nonie.

And the love was there, and the longer he was away, the fonder he was getting of her. One day, at noon, he came to a house with no windows facing south, where he saw a woman drawing sunshine in a sieve into the kitchen.

'Give me a sledge,' says he, and he broke a round hole in the south wall of the house and he fitted the sieve into it and made a nice window—a bit draughty maybe, but it left in the sunshine!

Another day he came to a place where he saw a woman blindfolding sheep to prevent 'em from going through a gap into a piece of rhy-grass she had.

'Wouldn't it be simpler,' he said to her, 'to build up the gap!'

'Can't you build it up yourself so!' says she. 'And I'll bring you out a bit to ate while you are doing it.'

He set to work and she went into the house, and broke white bread into hot milk and made what we call goody. A spoon of sugar on top that and children'd go mad for it. But it could hardly be considered a fit diet for a working man.

When she was bringing it out of the house, she was walking into the slanting sun, and looking back she saw her shadow.

'Who are you?' she said. 'Maybe it is hungry you are,' throwing back a spoonful of the goody. And as the shadow kept on with her she said, '*Crymonás* you must be starving.' So she kept throwing back spoonfuls of the goody to the shadow, till by the time she arrived where Haley was building the gap the dish was empty!

Haley gave her a look like a summons and gathered his legs out of the place.

The third day he came to a house, where he heard the farmer inside bawling his head off the same as the poor people used to be roaring long 'go when the quack German doctor used to be going around curing the rheumatics. The only difference being, that the quack German doctor had a musician outside the window blowing the bugle, so that his patients couldn't be heard crying—for that would be bad for business!

Haley ran into the house and there was the farmer's wife with an affair like a big flour bag uown over her husband's head, and she belting him away on top of the nut with a beetle. Such treatment! As Haley said, you wouldn't do it to a black Russian!

'You'll kill the man!' says he, 'or what are you doing that for!'

'That's a shirt I'm running up for my husband,' says the woman. 'And I'm making a hole on top of it for his head. I've to make two holes for the hands yet!'

'Give me a scissors,' says Haley. And he cut a hole on top of the bag, and the farmer's head popped out, and I can tell you that the man was relieved.

'My eyes are opened for me now,' says Haley. 'I thought the woman blindfolding the sheep, and the woman drawing sunshine in a sieve were bad, but for the height of contrariness you capped all!' A person don't know how well off he is in his own house, until he travels out and sees what other women are like.'

So he turned on his heel and went home to Nonie, and I suppose it was only the strangeness of marriage that upset her. In a while's time she gave up the capers and settled down to be a most sensible little *dailc* of a woman, proud and independent, thrifty and industrious, smiling and companionable, in other words, as priceless a little person as ever sat under a cow!

CHAPTER THIRTEEN

THE HEREAFTER

There's a thing there's no noise about now, and when we were young our hearts'd be up in our mouths if we heard there was one of 'em coming. It would be well publicised beforehand, you may say, and it would be a very dull man living in a very out of the way place that wouldn't hear of it. Then, when the time'd come the roads 'd be black with people going there: men, women and children, although some people'd say it was no place at all for children. Ye think now I'm talking about the circus. I am not then, but about the mission!

Once every five years the mission'd come here, and my neighbours'd be talking about it for three years before and two years after. For, no word of a lie, it did make an impression, and an impression that was needed in certain quarters. Well the vows that'd be made and the pledges that'd be so taken! Line after line of hardened old campaigners facing the altar rails the final Sunday. Everyone'd be so changed you'd swear that from that out judges'd have to hang up their wigs, and publicans'd have to go selling shirt buttons.

Two holy fathers that used come here, and even though of saintly appearance, well versed you may say in every description of villainy. They'd light the chapel with language, bringing their voices away down very low, and then making a tremendous shout that'd frighten the living daylights out of everyone. People used be afraid to go up near the altar. And we'll say a shy man sitting there, if the holy father fixed his eye on him, and he in a rage, the poor man'd pass out!

Even down near the door where we used to be, you'd be shivering in your shoes, for each night they'd go from one evil doing to another, from the sins of life to death, from death to judgment, and from judgment, as was only natural, to the place below! Oh glory! The fires of hell'd be described down to the very last detail, the smoke and the steam and the gnashing of teeth! Poor old women sitting there in the chapel, no more sin on 'em than the child in the cradle, only trying to make ends meet, and the tears rolling down their cheeks at the thought of all those people suffering on the hobs of hell for all eternity.

And I'll never forget one night, there was this woman from out The Bower, a hat on her, and there she was as unconcerned as if she was at a football match. Of course the holy father couldn't help but notice her—'twas the big man that was on the same night. And when she was going out the gate after, 'twas the small man said Benediction, the big man was there before her.

'How is it,' says he, 'my good woman that you were so unmoved by all the suffering in hell's flames?'

'Yerra father,' says she, 'I'm not from this parish at all!'

And they used to travel from parish to parish after the missioners—some people can take an awful hammering!

One night the sermon'd be given over to drink; another night to company keeping and so on. There'd be some sins mentioned and if the people were given a free hand they wouldn't know how to go about committing 'em! But coming in to the second week we'd all be coming closer to grace, and the final night would be glorious. Old lads there with no more note in 'em no more than a crow trying to sing. 'Never will we sin again!' And the great blaze of light when all the candles were lit for the renouncing of the devil. I can tell you if that bucko put in an appearance that night he'd get a belt of a fist as quick as lightening! Such fervour!

Monday morning we'd all return to normal life. And I'll never forget this Monday morning, I was over here at the forge putting slippers on the mare. There was a big crowd there and the only topic of conversation was the mission. And some people held that after all that was said we were given a very poor inkling as to what heaven was like. Well, they admitted heaven was mentioned earlier on, but at that time very little hope was held out for the people. But now that they all expected to go there, they were wondering what sort of place it was. Would they have to work there! What would the weather be like!

And we'll say for instance the man that was married twice here, which one of 'em would he be walking out with in heaven? He couldn't be walking out with two of 'em—or maybe it was alright in heaven to have two—they didn't know!

The blacksmith was wondering would there be a public house there where we could go in and sit down, he said, and talk to the neighbours. Well, there was this fellow there, a good footballer in his day, until he got broke in the wind, and wound up carrying the *ganseys*. Heaven wouldn't be much in his eyes anyway, unless they had an occasional football match.

'Maybe,' says he, 'we'd get up a team and travel out!'

Another man there used to scrape a bit on the fiddle—he wasn't much good. He'd like heaven to be a place where he'd meet all these musicians and they'd be exchanging tunes.

> I have a bonnet trimmed with blue,
> Why don't you wear it, sure I do.
> Why don't you wear it when you can
> Going to the dance with your young man.

Dance! That was it. All the young people said heaven wouldn't be much to write home about if there was no dancing.

Now there was an old lad sitting up on the hob, never opened his mouth during all this, only making curly cues in the ashes with his walking cane.

'*Sea*, dance!' says he with a smile, 'from what we heard about heaven in the chapel during the past two weeks, there won't be enough there from this parish to make up a half set!'

And did the people pay heed to the missioners? Oh-h-h they did! It had a very beneficial effect. Although some took it too serious so that it played a bit on their mind. There was this woman and she took the sermons on company keeping very much to heart. She was married but the husband died and left her with an only son.

She brought up the son very strict. Even from a

very early age he wouldn't be allowed talk to girls. He wouldn't be let go anywhere girls'd be. He was never at a dance. He had to keep away from all places of temptation, so that he wouldn't be the cause of bringing disgrace on her or having her name called from the altar. The result of all this was that he grew up backward—going the opposite side of the road when he saw girls coming! — John the Shyman people used to call him.

One Sunday after a mission, he was going the near way through a wood with his mother, and they met a young couple linking arms together!

'What are they up to, Mammy?' says he to the mother.

'Don't mind them now!' says she, 'that's only a brother and sister going to the holy well, praying.'

He had his doubts about that, especially when he saw the two lovers fall into a bed of bluebells.

'Look the other way!' says the mother. 'Oh,' says he, 'no wonder the missioner is making tapes on the altar!'

When his mother died he had no one to do anything for him, and this poor man's daughter used to come housekeeping. Now, look we'll be charitable, maybe she was put up to it for he had a fine farm of land! Anyway she got around him and they had to get married. Look at that after all his mother's warning.

He had nearly to be tied to bring him to the altar, afraid of his life of the P. P., but nothing was said for the P. P. didn't know. But six months after when the wife presented him with a big belter of a baby boy—John the Shyman nearly went out of his mind.

Two days after was the christening, and when he

heard he'd have to bring the child to the chapel, rather than confront Father Furnane, he took to the hill. The father-in-law wasn't long bringing him back. The horse was tackled, and when the wife's mother, holding the child, was made comfortable sitting on a *gabhál* of straw in the body of the car, John the Shyman and the two witnesses to the baptism sat in and they drove off to the chapel.

Now, the parish priest we had here at the time, Father Furnane, had a strict rule concerning baptism. It would take place at three o'clock on the dot, and if you weren't there at that time you'd have a little pagan in the house for another while. The baptism party were very much aware of this so they were urging John to hurry the horse, for if they were late Father Furnane 'd ate the face of 'em.

By the time the band was retrieved, the wife's mother and the child taken out of the car, the horse untackled, the wheel taken off, the band put on it, bits of kippens wedged between the band and the felloes to tighten it, the wheel put back under the car, the horse tackled, and the wife's mother and the child put sitting on the straw, I can tell you a good bit of the day was gone.

Then too because of the precarious condition of the band speed was out of the question, so that Father Furnane was gone into the sacristy by the time they arrived at the chapel. But the wife's mother, brazen enough, faith, took her place with the child and the two sponsors at the baptismal font. John the Shyman ducked down behind a pillar to hide!

The parish clerk, oh a very officious fellow, with a long black coat buttoned up to his chin—ideas above his station! Sure one time at confirmation he nearly got a parish from the bishop. Of course hearing the baptismal party arriving late, he marched out from the sacristy, looking every bit as furious as Father Furnane, and pointing to where the little child was he said:

'Who is responsible for this?'

And John the Shyman putting his head around the pillar said:

'It won't happen again, Father!'

GLOSSARY

For the benefit of the readers unfamiliar with the Irish language this list of Irish words (or words derived from Irish) is appended. In translating we have endeavoured not only to give verbal equivalences but also to convey something of the flavour of the meaning of the original Irish.

A mhico — sonny
A Thiarna — Lord
Agus ag trácht dúinn ar uisce — and talking about water
Árus — grand dwelling
An buile tobac — tabacco madness
Bacáns — hinges
Bhí an Ghaelige go blasta aice siúd, agus is i nGaeilge a
  bheidís ag caint i gcónaí — She had fluent Irish, and it
  was in Irish they always spoke
Bóthairín — boreen (by-road)
Brúscar — fine pieces
Cábúis — nook
Carraig — rock
Circín — chicken
Cliamháin isteach — son-in-law (living with wife's parents)
Cnocán — hillock
Craiceann is a luach — the skin and the price of it
Creachaills — gnarled pieces of wood
Crónán — humming
Croí an diabhail — by the devil's heart
Críost go deo! — Eternal Christ!
Crymonás — O Crikey
Cúl gháirdín — back garden
Cúlóg — one who rides behind another on horseback
Cupóg — dock leaf

Cuir uait an chaint — stop talking

Cúis gháire chughainn — what a joke!

Dailc — low sized, stout

Dia Linn — God be with us

D'réir an seana chultúr — according to custom

Fág an Bealach — Make way : this phrase is used in the sense 'knocking sparks out of the flagstones'.

Gabháil — armful

Gaisce — great deed

Ganseys — jersies

Garsún — boy

Go brónach — sorrowful

Grá mo chrói — lovingly

Groísach — embers

I gcúntas Dé a grá ghil — in God's name, love

Leabaidh na mbocht — the poor bed

Lúbán — a bent thing

Mar eadh! — indeed!

Méaróg — a thin hay rope, made by one person

Mo léir! — Alas!

Mo lén cráite — woeful sorrow

Múnlach — animal urine

Nóiníns — daisies

Ologón — lamenting

Pé in Éirinn é — however

Réiteoir — pipe cleaner

Sceón — terror

Sea — yes

Smathán — a good measure

Solus na bhflaitheas dúinn go léir — the light of heaven on us all

Spág — a long flat foot

Suarachy — small

Súgán — a straw rope

Súilíns — bubbles
Tamall — while
Tanam an diúcs — your soul to the devil
Taoscán — a little drop
Taoscing — pouring
Tráithnín — a strong blade of grass
Trí na céile — confused